WHILE YOU WERE GONE

MARK GILLESPIE

INKUBATOR
BOOKS

Published by Inkubator Books
www.inkubatorbooks.com

Copyright © 2025 by Mark Gillespie

Mark Gillespie has asserted his right to be identified as the author of this work.

ISBN (eBook): 978-1-83756-569-6
ISBN (Paperback): 978-1-83756-570-2
ISBN (Hardback): 978-1-83756-571-9

WHILE YOU WERE GONE is a work of fiction. People, places, events, and situations are the product of the author's imagination. Any resemblance to actual persons, living or dead is entirely coincidental.

No part of this book may be reproduced, stored in any retrieval system, or transmitted by any means without the prior written permission of the publisher.

*Dedicated to the memory of
Walter Gillespie
(1947–2024)
Dad xx*

PROLOGUE
GLENCOE, SCOTLAND

The old cottage is ablaze. Thick, black smoke billows from the roof and disappears up into a starless sky.

I stand and watch while the vicious heat claws at my skin. It's a bonfire that no one beside the loch or at the foot of the mountains expected to see tonight. Certainly, I didn't. It feels like I'm trapped inside a giant oven, and although I have the option of walking away to safer ground, I don't.

I can't.

I want to watch.

Above the thunderous roar of the flames, I still hear the sound of the house sitter's voice. Playing over and over again like a broken record. Just for me.

I'll take good care of things.

Don't worry.

I'll take good care of things.

It's Martha Hunt's voice, and it won't leave me. Twisted and demonic, echoing in my mind. Her voice drowning out not only the flames but also the approaching sirens as they draw nearer to the old cottage. Every cell, every atom of my being is infested with Martha Hunt. I'll close my eyes at night and see her because she's a part of me now. Floating around inside me. That voice. Those blank eyes.

I'll take good care of things.

Why us? It's a question that will haunt me for the rest of my life, yet if I'm looking for a profound or fatalistic answer, there isn't one. Why did she have to walk into our lives that day? The answer is simple. Because we needed a house sitter, that's all. Correction – we needed a *last-minute* house sitter because Dan and I were setting off on a much-needed holiday to visit his friends. It was a therapeutic retreat, at least for me.

We settled for Martha because we wanted a house sitter, *needed* a house sitter, as quickly as possible. We opened our home to her because we chose to, not because the devil opened his trapdoor and let her out.

Although, I still have doubts.

Speaking of doubts, they were there from the beginning. A voice in my head telling me – *screaming* at me – that we were rushing, making a mistake. I ignored it, and the voice didn't go away. *There's something not right about her.* Ignored it. I knew that was wrong and that it's never a good idea to use a last-minute replacement to take care of your house and your cherished pets. But I took the voice in my head as nothing more than a silly bout of nerves, that's all. I put it down to the usual last-minute, pre-holiday panic, especially as we were in a hurry, and I was exhausted from all the cleaning and fussing and packing.

Don't worry. I'll take good care of things.

I remember how Martha followed those words (and so many others) with a high-pitched laugh like she knew it was all a big joke from the beginning. A hyena's laugh. A taunting cackle that felt like glass shattering inside my head.

Despite the fact we were rushing, I told myself she was harmless. That she was funny and quirky and interesting. How did I get it so wrong? She looked like someone fun and offbeat with her big, permed hair and that flowery cardigan she always wore. The big glasses, the smile and, yes, the laugh sometimes too. She was punctual, and I've always liked that in a person. A bit eccentric, perhaps. Strange. Frumpy.

But harmless.

Here I am. Still trying to make sense of this. Still trying to understand how it came from needing an emergency house sitter to standing outside a burning cottage in the Highlands.

I feel alone despite the incoming sirens. Tonight feels like the end of the world.

We chose her, and that's all there is to it. That's why she came into our lives. I was worried about the pets and the house, but not worried enough to delay our holiday and be more thorough about who we were letting into our lives. I needn't have worried about the pets or the house in the end. They were fine. Alive and still standing. It was me whom Martha came for. *Me*. It was everything else that went wrong after we came home early and found her the way we did.

But ... harmless.

All we wanted was a good, reliable house sitter. All I wanted was a nice holiday to forget about the anniversary of Mum's death. Was it too much to ask?

I'll stay close to the burning cottage. The smoke is overpowering. It feels like being skinned alive very slowly, but I'm not ready to leave yet. The firefighters will be here soon, and they'll drag me away kicking and screaming. Or maybe it's not the fire department. Could be the police or an ambulance, and maybe that'll give me a little more time.

Time to watch. To be sure that it's over.

I haven't even begun to think about the aftermath of all this. What am I supposed to tell these people when they sit me down and ask the inevitable – *what happened?* How will I tell this story? The story of Martha Hunt, the woman whom I will never be free of.

I cough and grimace. But I won't take a backwards step. Won't take my eyes off the cottage until it's beyond my control.

That sick, twisted bitch. She lied to us.

She said she'd take good care of things.

PART 1

THE HOUSE SITTER

CHAPTER ONE

Dan picks up the remote control and turns the volume on the TV down.

"Let's go on holiday," he says.

Prior to this sudden announcement, we were sitting on the couch, watching a true-crime documentary on Netflix. Some serial-killer anthology series that isn't grabbing either one of us judging by the way Dan keeps looking at his phone, and I'm concentrating more on folding clothes and putting them in a basket of fresh laundry.

"What?" I ask.

He inches towards me on the couch. Getting closer is Dan's usual way of letting me know that he's serious about something. Still, I ask the question.

"Are you serious?"

"Yes, I'm serious. Let's do it. I think we need a change of scenery."

"Oh really."

This hasn't exactly come out of nowhere. It's a sensitive

time of year for me, to say the least. It's the anniversary of Mum's death. She died on November fifteenth, thirty-two years ago, and even the sound of it – *November fifteenth* – is enough to make me go cold. I was seven when it happened, and God knows it still haunts me, both the fact that she died and the way she died.

Sometimes I don't know which one is worse.

"We can't just go on holiday," I say.

Dan coughs into the back of his hand. Clears his throat. "Why not?"

"Well, you're coming down with something, for a start."

"Eh?"

"The cough."

"I'm fine. My body's just anticipating the onslaught of another Scottish winter."

"Bull."

"It's true. I'm fine."

I put down the T-shirts I've been folding. As I do, Billie Jean, our cat, is doing her best to sabotage my efforts to keep cat hairs off the clothes. Where I see clean clothes, she sees an irresistible bed. After she tries to hop into the basket for the tenth time, I lift her and put her onto the floor. She looks up at me, twitching her tail in disgust. Then she struts away, sulking.

I start folding T-shirts again. On TV, a blonde girl who survived a serial killer by jumping out of a moving van talks about survivor's guilt.

"Well?" Dan asks.

"Well what?"

"Why can't we just take a holiday if we want to?"

"Because we haven't talked about it. Where did this

come from, anyway? Is it because of … because of the anniversary?"

I never quite know what to call it. *Anniversary* sounds like such a happy occasion and doesn't seem right when we're talking about the single worst moment of my life. Still, anniversary is what I call it.

He smiles. "We're talking about it now."

"Dan—"

He pushes himself off the couch and slides the washing basket along the coffee table, making room to sit down in front of me. My arms flop to the sides. He's serious about this. I can tell by the way he arches his eyebrows into two hairy ticks. He leans in close, almost like he's coming in for a kiss.

"C'mon. What do you think?"

I shrug. "Like it's that easy."

"It *is* easy," he says in a pleading voice. "We're not talking about going to the moon, Ang. It's a one- or two-week holiday. We deserve it."

"There's still a lot to do."

His hands shoot up like he's surrendering.

"You're right. There are things we need to do. Arrangements we have to make, but it's not *that* hard to do any of them. Not if we really want to go, and right now, I think we both want and need to go."

"Hmm."

"What do you say?"

My mind races back and forth. I'm searching for excuses to throw at him. Excuses that will put this conversation to bed once and for all. That's us, Mr Positive and Miss Negative. Still, I guess it works. We're together, aren't we? Dan might have days when he sounds like a walking self-help book, but he has a way of making even the most predictable of phrases work in the moment. That's one of the reasons I fell for him. He makes me feel safe, and he does it better than any pill or drink, and God knows I tried enough of those back in my late teens and early twenties.

I was drawn to Dan the first time I met him at the group therapy sessions we both attended. Specifically, it was a trauma and PTSD support group, and there's been variations of these sessions in and around Glasgow over the years. They've been going on for decades. Open to everyone. Run by volunteers. It's no big deal – just somewhere informal for people to go if they need to talk, listen or be around that sort of healing space. I did one-on-one sessions with a therapist when I was growing up with my aunt and uncle, and they were a lot to cope with. I've been going on and off to these group sessions for years to help cope with the way I fall apart every November – my couple of weeks of madness. Sometimes on, mostly off. But the good thing about the sessions, no matter who's holding them, is that the door is open. It can be weeks, months or years since your last visit, but everyone is welcome back.

Sooner or later, I always go back.

It's been eleven years since Dan and I met in one such session in a community centre in the west end of Glasgow. He'd been struggling with his sister's suicide. That happened a full year before Dan plucked up the courage to walk into one of the open sessions. He was the one who found Amy, who was only twenty-four years old when she died. She was a vet nurse who'd succumbed to compassion fatigue, which I learned is emotional exhaustion from exposure to traumatic situations. It's basically burnout. Moral distress. It's not uncommon in vets and vet nurses, who also have to take a lot of crap from people about money. Dan and his parents were crushed when Amy died. It took Dan a year to admit that he'd still nowhere near processed it, and although he wasn't willing to go and see a professional one-on-one, he did relent after a friend advised him to try the open therapy sessions in a Partick community centre.

That's where our story began.

Two broken people, drawn to one another across a circle of chairs and sad stories. A lot of sad stories. It's not an easy place to be, but it can be rewarding if you stick it out and get past that initial resistance. The weight of sorrow in those rooms is immense, yet, as hard as it is to talk about some of the things we've lived through, I always come out feeling lighter. Like some of that weight has been removed; I don't know how, but it just happens. Perseverance rewarded, I suppose.

I'd been attending on and off for a few months at the Partick community centre when Dan first showed up. I remember that night well. It was summer. He was boyish and shy. Still, he spoke that first night and said he was hopeful that trying something new would help him deal with the nightmares. Nightmares that hadn't subsided since he'd walked into his sister's bedroom that morning.

I didn't want to tell Dan, after we'd gotten to know one another, that nothing could stop the nightmares. Therapy was like a balm. It soothed but never got to the root of the matter. At least that's how it was for me. I hoped I was wrong and that maybe Dan's experience would be different to mine. I suspected his nightmares would remain but that they'd come around less frequently. And with less intensity.

It was hard for him, those first few sessions. I could tell

that he didn't want to be there. The weariness in his eyes and the awkward lingering at the door before each session as he debated whether or not to stay. I know that feeling. There are a lot of people like that at the open sessions. Every November, I'm the same.

It took him a few weeks before he was able to really start talking about Amy. He spoke about her in a way that made me feel like I knew her. He spoke about her like she was still alive and still making all those plans to travel to her beloved Japan and to run at least one marathon in her lifetime. It wasn't easy to listen, and it was a lot harder for Dan to bare his soul like he did. Not long afterwards, we went out for our first drink together. And we didn't speak once about our family tragedies. That was for therapy.

That first date, if that's what it was, went well. It clicked. *We* clicked.

Now, here we are. Living together in a little house eight miles northeast of Glasgow. We have a cat and dog, and for me, it's the first romantic relationship of my adult life that's transcended the superficial.

Dan doesn't go to therapy anymore. He got everything out of it that he needed. It helped him to cope better with Amy's death, and while it's never going to be easy for him to live with what happened, he deals with it much better than I deal with what happened to Mum. He doesn't turn into a basket case once every twelve months.

"Where would we go?" I ask, warming to the idea of a holiday but not wanting to make it too obvious to Dan.

Who am I kidding? Dan sees it alright. He knows my guard is coming down.

"Does it even matter?"

"That's a dumb question."

"Angie," he says, "when was the last time we went anywhere? When was the last time we just dropped everything and did something for ourselves?"

I shrug. We've talked about a lot of trips, but we haven't pulled the trigger. Laziness, money – there's always an excuse hanging around if you want one.

"I don't know."

"Think."

"Barcelona?"

"Right," Dan says. "That was over three years ago."

It feels more like ten.

"So where *would* we go? I don't even know if my passport is up to date."

"Don't get excited. We're not going to Brazil or anything like that." I see hints of a mischievous smile forming on his face. A twinkle in his eye. "But it just so happens you won't need a passport for this trip."

"Spit it out."

He nods. "We have been invited up to Glencoe for the week."

"What? Glencoe? In the—?"

"Highlands."

I frown. "Who invited us up there?"

"My old uni mates," Dan says. "Jonny and Michael Laing."

"The brothers?"

Dan grins. "The *rich* brothers."

"I didn't know you'd kept in touch with the Laings."

"Just online for the most part," he says. "Social media and sometimes an email back and forth. But we've always talked about holding a reunion somewhere down the line. We just never got around to it."

"A reunion? Were you that close?"

"Best buds back in the day. There was me, Jonny, Michael and Gordy. The fabulous foursome. Well, that's not exactly what the teachers called us."

"Is Gordy invited to this reunion?"

"Of course. But he lives in New Zealand, and the last I heard, he's got more kids than a rugby team. Don't know if it's that easy for him to get over here."

He playfully taps the back of my hand with his finger.

"You want to see the house they've got up there, Ang. It's glorious. It's this big mansion sitting right on the banks of Loch Leven. It's surrounded by mountains, and the wildlife is incredible. It's like something out of a film, I'm telling you."

I smile, more for Dan's sake. "Just how rich are these guys?"

"Filthy rich," Dan says without hesitation. "Not that Jonny or Michael earned a single penny of it. All the money, the *real* money, comes from their grandfather's business. Electronics. Computers. That sort of thing. The company made it big in the eighties, and when I say big, I mean BIG."

He bursts out laughing.

"Who cares about all that? We've been invited to stay at the house for a week. Jonny and Michael live in London these days, but they're going up there with their girlfriends. I'd love to see them again. And I think it'd be good for you. What do you say?"

He reaches over and gives my shoulder a gentle squeeze.

"We're allowed to stop once in a while, Ang."

"I don't know," I say with a sigh.

"C'mon," Dan says. "This is exactly what you need right now. I've been thinking about it for a while."

"Thinking about what?"

"That we should make this a habit around the ... around the ... you know, the anniversary."

"Make a habit of what?"

"Getting away. Taking a holiday. Doing something for ourselves."

I look down at the floor. There are still plenty of T-shirts to fold, but I've lost the rhythm I was in.

"Are you okay?" Dan asks.

"Hmm."

"I know it's a tough time of year, Ang," he says in a soothing voice. "But let's try to turn this thing around, starting this year with the Laings. The loch, the mountains, the peace and quiet. It'll be fun. From this year onwards, let's make mid-November something to look forward to instead of something to dread."

I brave another smile. "What about my writing?"

"You can write while you're up there. Who knows – you might be inspired by the setting."

"What about my delivery work?"

"You deliver food for an app at night," he says. "You're not obliged to go out and work unless you want to."

I narrow my eyes. "Dan, I'm trying to earn my own money until I make it as a writer. It's important to me."

"I know. But you've been working like a maniac. That's what you always do around the anniversary, long days and even longer nights, and I'm saying it'll be better if we just get out of Glasgow. A change of scene and all that."

"I don't know."

"I think you do know."

"Oh really?"

I can almost hear the wheels in his brain turning as he

gives me the hard stare. He picks up the remote again and this time turns the TV off. I was kind of enjoying the background true-crime ambience but whatever.

"Something else is bothering you," he says. "What is it?"

I hesitate before giving a half-hearted shrug. "I've been thinking about the group therapy sessions. Maybe I'll go back for a while. See if it helps."

"Where?"

"Strathclyde uni."

He nods. "Do you know what the best therapy in the world is, Ang?"

"Wouldn't happen to be a mansion in Glencoe, would it?"

He laughs. "I was going to say Mother Nature and her lochs and fresh mountain air, but sure – a mansion in Glencoe it is. And hey, you can always go to the sessions when we come back. They're not going anywhere."

"Tempting," I say.

Dan clenches a fist in victory and holds it aloft. "Yes! That settles it. We leave on Friday morning."

"Friday? *This* Friday?"

"Absolutely. We're living on the edge now, Ang. Okay, it's only a three-hour drive from Glasgow to Glencoe. But—"

"But?"

"How about we take it real slow? There's a lot of good things in between here and the Laing house. We could spend a night in one of the hotels at Loch Lomond. See the sights. Then we travel north and do some hiking around Glen Etive. From there, it's a quick drive up to the Laing mansion on Sunday morning. That's when the Laings are arriving at the house, so it'll be perfect timing."

"Sounds like you've got it all planned," I say.

"I've been thinking about it."

"Have you? Have you really thought it *all* through?"

Dan frowns. "What do you mean?"

It's my turn to pull out the hard stare. "You're forgetting something."

"Like what?"

As if on cue, Billie Jean leaps into the basket of freshly washed clothes. *Whatever*, I think, watching as she kneads one of my favourite T-shirts. I should have stopped worrying about cat hairs on my clothes a long time ago.

"We have fur babies," I remind Dan. "One cat, one demanding dog. You weren't planning to just up and leave them to fend for themselves, were you?"

"Of course not."

"So what's the plan?"

"Don't worry," Dan says, opening the Google app on his phone. "That's what kennels and catteries are for. I'll sort it out."

I wag a finger back and forth in his direction. "Billie Jean doesn't do well in catteries. She's staying here. In the house."

"She is?"

"They both are."

"In that case," Dan says, "we need a house sitter. Someone who'll come here and live in. Okay, okay. How hard can it be?"

"On two days' notice? Pretty hard. Possibly impossible."

Dan's face wrinkles in concentration. I sense he's more than a little rattled under that cool exterior. "Can you think of anyone?"

"Me? I've only just found out about this holiday."

"Right. What about your friend? What's-her-name? The

redhead – is it Sophie? Sofia? She's a vet, isn't she? She'd be perfect."

"She's got a board exam coming up."

Dan grimaces, and those deep grooves crinkle his forehead again. Then he clicks his fingers. "I know! My mum's friend Jean. She loves animals. She used to be a dogwalker back in the day. If Mum gives me her number, then—"

"No."

"What? Why not?"

"I met Jean at your mum's garage sale last year," I say. "Remember? There's no way she's up to it."

"Why not?"

"Brogan's a big, young Labrador. And Jean's what? In her late eighties? Even if she did want to house-sit for us, we can't just roll up and ask her out of the blue. We haven't spoken to her in years."

Dan nods, accepting defeat. "Seems like all our friends have kids. Can't ask any of them either."

"Yep."

"So where does that leave us?"

I almost say it. That we can't go to the Laing house and that we'll have to put off going anywhere until we make proper, *unhurried* plans. But there is one option that neither one of us has mentioned yet.

"It leaves us in the hands of a professional house-sitting agency," I say. "If we're serious about this, we need to go online, suss it out and see if anyone's available at short notice. Very short notice, I might add."

Dan scratches the stubble on his chin. It's a hard, raking noise that creeps me out. "Okay. Let's do that."

"It's going to cost us," I tell him. "That's if someone's

available. Usually, these people are booked out months in advance."

Well, the good ones are.

Dan's already browsing the options on Google. "There must be someone out there who can do it."

"We'll see," I tell him. "But, Dan?"

He doesn't look up. "Hmm?"

"Whoever it is, they have to be perfect."

CHAPTER TWO

I'm waiting at the front door when her car turns into the driveway. I hear the soft crunch of the tyres as they roll over gravel. It's a sound I've always loved. Reminds me of my aunt Rose coming home from work and how we'd make dinner together and watch TV with the cats on our laps. That was a tradition that went on for years. I'll always love that sound, and today, I'm hoping it's a good sign. I'm hoping it means that we're bringing the right person into our life. Someone that I can trust with Billie and Brogan, not to mention with the house itself.

The car stops. The engine goes quiet. It feels like a long time passes before the driver's door opens.

She's here.

The house sitter.

It's going to be fine, I tell myself. I can't believe how fast my heart is beating, and it feels like I'm going on a first date or about to walk into an important exam.

It's going to be fine. It's going to be great.

She's on the path, walking away from her car. *Clip-clop. Clip-clop.* Sounds like a small horse approaching the front door.

"Martha's here!" I call to Dan in a shrill voice. Not so loud that she might hear me from outside.

His voice reaches me from the other end of the hallway. "Almost done."

I've ordered him to empty the silver bin in the bathroom. I don't know why I did that. Even when Martha does use the bathroom, I doubt she'll judge us for having a bin that's overflowing with fragments of toilet paper, dental floss and cotton buds.

She knocks at the door. Three times.

My heart is pounding.

Here we go, I think. *Please let this work out.*

I wait a few seconds before answering, just so she doesn't think I've been standing behind the door waiting for her to arrive. That would reek of desperation. I even thump my feet off the floor to make it sound like I'm hurrying towards the door from somewhere else in the house.

"Coming!" I yell, wondering if I've overdone the air freshener.

Too late now.

I open the door, and Martha's hand is already outstretched. Quite a large hand, I notice. Fat fingers. Lots of rings.

"I'm so pleased to meet you," she says in a smooth, velvety voice. She's grinning from ear to ear. "I'm Martha Hunt."

I take her hand. Her skin is soft and spongy.

"I'm Angie. Pleased to meet you too."

I beckon her inside.

"Please, come in."

"Thank you very much. Looks like we're going to have some rain today, hmm?"

"I think so."

I lead her towards the living room. My first impression is that I like her, and I'm a big believer when it comes to first impressions. Instinct. Intuition. These things are far more important than CVs or qualifications. Well, that's what I'm telling myself, anyway.

The word quirky leaps to mind, and cosy isn't far behind it.

Quirky, cosy Martha.

She's a striking-looking woman, sporting a big eighties-style perm that you'd have to be blind to miss in a crowd. The agency website states that Martha is in her early sixties, yet she dresses like a much older woman with her buttoned-up, greyish cardigan with its swirling floral pattern on the front. Her shoes look like slippers. She wears oversized glasses, and I notice that behind those Coke-bottle lenses, the eyes are tiny. Cartoonishly small, like shrunken dots.

I put the kettle on, and the three of us sit down for a getting-to-know-you chat. The atmosphere is informal despite the fact that we hired Martha through a professional agency. Truth be told, it wasn't the best agency. Their website was clunky, but the reviews for their sitters were mostly positive. Dan and I read through them all at my insistence. Hopefully, they're real and not ones the agency wrote themselves. Martha was one of the few sitters available on such short notice, and I suppose, from the description, she sounded like a safe bet. Dan and I liked her because she was older. A lot of the younger sitters who came up in the search just seem to be passing through on holiday, looking for a place to stay while they explore the area. Most of those weren't available for this week anyway, and even if they had been, they weren't the sort of people I want to leave with my dog and cat. I want someone who sounds like they want to be here.

We make chit-chat, but the real test for me is how Billie Jean and Brogan behave around Martha. So far, so good. They're curious. Not shying away either, which for Billie Jean is a good sign. She usually runs a mile from strangers and stays away for a good twenty minutes at least.

Don't they say cats are a good judge of character?

"Good boy," Martha says, rubbing Brogan on the head and back. He seems to be enjoying it, judging by the way his tail is wagging. "You're a good boy, aren't you? Yes, you are. Yes, you are!"

Dan and I exchange encouraging looks. He gives a subtle thumbs-up gesture when Martha isn't looking.

This might just be okay, I tell myself.

We also have to remember that this meeting works both ways. Martha's looking at us every bit as much as we're looking at her. Right now, she's deciding whether this is a job she wants to take on, especially as it's short notice and it'll take her away from whatever else she's got going on in her life.

"Would you like another cup of tea?" I ask, noticing that Martha's cup is empty.

"Not for me, dear," she says. "Tea goes right through me, and I'll spend half the day sitting on the toilet. Pissing my brains out!"

She lets out a wild shriek of laughter. I can't help but join in.

Quirky, cosy AND funny.

We make more small talk while Martha continues to interact with the pets, who've settled well in her presence. Then, seeing as how Dan isn't leading the charge, I decide to ask the big question.

"So," I say, smiling in Martha's direction, "what do you think?"

The living room falls silent. Dan sits on the other armchair, rigid and tall, like he's about to receive his sentence after a murder trial. Martha stops scratching Brogan's ear and looks over at me. It feels like an hour passes before she says anything.

"About the job?"

"Yes. Are you interested in housesitting for us?"

That regretful look on her face. *Oh shit*, I think to myself. *We've lost her. She's going to say no.* I have no idea what did it. Was it me? Was it Dan? She seems to love the pets, so why wouldn't she house sit for us? Is it the house?

It's me. I did something. I said something. I'm too eager, and she can smell it a mile away.

She looks at us both. "Umm—"

That sudden high-pitched squeal of laughter fills the room again. Feels like it's powerful enough to take the roof off the house and every other roof of every other house in the street too. She rocks back and forth on the chair, slapping her knees. "Oh, your faces. Both of you. I'm just winding you up, love."

Dan grins. "Oh, right."

I laugh because I don't know what else to do.

Dan and I are both on edge because, in all likelihood, it'll be too late to make alternate arrangements, and that'll be the end of the trip to Glencoe. A trip that, once I got my head around it, I've been very much looking forward to. Dan was right – I both want and need it. I'd be gutted if we lost it now.

"So?" Dan asks. "You're up for it?"

Martha glances around the living room, perhaps weighing up any last-minute considerations in her mind. She looks at me, eyes shimmering with excitement.

"I'll do it."

Dan punches the air. "Yes!"

I breathe a sigh of relief, but I make an effort not to look as desperate as Dan. After a minute or so, I'm up on my feet, hurrying towards the kitchen. I open the top drawer beside the sink and pull out the notes – the *extensive* notes – that I've written and printed out about Billie Jean and Brogan. Their care sheets, I call them. Dan calls it my first novel. Yes, there *is* a lot here, but they've both got their particular needs, and Billie Jean is on daily oral medication for her joints. They also have specific behaviour patterns that any good sitter would want to know about. Right? I'm not a fruit loop – I'm just thorough. It's all here in one handy guide. With pictures.

I've written up notes about the house in a separate document. We live in a rental, and it's quite old, and a lot of the stuff in it is a bit old, for that matter. It'll be useful for Martha to know where the Wi-Fi works best and the fact that the floorboards creak, which on a windy night makes it sound like there's an intruder in the house. One of the fire alarms is temperamental, too. I didn't realise how much there was to write about until I started writing it. If it was up to Dan, there'd be a Post-it note on the fridge and nothing else.

I take my notes into the living room. Martha can take them home with her, and it'll give her a head start for the weekend.

"All in all," Dan says, offering Martha a biscuit from the tin on the coffee table, "we'll be gone for one week exactly. So we're back on the following Friday morning. Mid-afternoon at the very latest."

Martha lifts a shortbread finger off the plate. I think it's her fourth. As she eats, she laughs off Brogan's pleading stare for her to share.

"Good boy," she says. "You're a good boy, aren't you? You love your auntie Martha."

Auntie Martha, I think.

This could definitely work.

She ruffles Brogan's head while I run through some of the things I've written down. One of my big concerns is the doggy door we have installed in the living room. It's used by both pets, and it leads out into the back garden. I've jotted down how the latches can be a little bit tricky and how I always make sure the door is locked from the inside after six o'clock because I don't want Billie Jean outside in the dark. There are foxes around here. I know I'm talking a lot. Throwing too much at Martha too soon, but she just nods while I run down the list. She'll be fine once she reads the notes.

Breathe, Angie, I remind myself.

"The fire alarm in the living room sometimes goes off for no apparent reason," I say. "It's kind of annoying, and it freaks Brogan out. I just take out the batteries and leave it for an hour. We'll have to replace it."

I look at Dan.

He nods. "Yeah, we'll get on that. *I'll* get on that."

I'm still talking so fast. Still running through things on the list. There are so many things to mention, and I'm aware we only have today and Friday morning to speak to Martha. Show her the ropes.

"No problem," Martha says when I'm done. "I'll study the notes like my life depends on it."

"Thanks," I say. "I really appreciate it."

I hand her the sheets of paper, stapled together and contained within a plastic folder. Dan offers her another biscuit. She takes the last shortbread finger.

"And once again," Dan says, sitting back down, "apologies for the short notice. We wouldn't usually be this unorganised when it comes to going on holiday."

"That's fine," Martha says, chewing happily. Brogan sits at her feet and stares at her. I tell him out loud (for Martha's sake, really) that he's not allowed to stare at people while they eat. "I didn't have much on in terms of work anyway. If I'm not housesitting, I'm staying with my daughter in Cumbernauld. She's got a little motor home in the leisure village. But I'm happy to come here for a week. I'll consider it a wee bonus job, and anyway, I'm not fully booked up until February. That's when my regulars try to escape the last bite of the Scottish winter."

I nod. "I bet you're popular."

"I am," she says.

Martha doesn't stay long after that. We make arrangements and let her know what time is best to come over on Friday morning. Then I walk her to the door, thanking her again for accepting the job. I must've thanked Martha at least fifty times since she walked through the door.

"See you Friday," she says. And she rubs my arm. "I'm so happy to help you guys out. You're just lovely, the pair of you."

"Thanks, Martha."

Fifty-one.

When she's gone, I close the door and let out a loud sigh of relief that contains half my bodyweight. I hear the chirp of her car alarm. The door slamming shut, the engine waking up, and then she's reversing down the driveway.

"That went well," Dan says, walking through into the hallway. He comes over, and we embrace.

"You're sweating," he says, wiping my brow.

"I know."

"But it was good," he says. "It did go well."

"It did," I say. "Didn't it?"

Dan nods. "She's perfect. The pets will be fine, and the house will be fine. We can go on the road now and relax."

"It had to be perfect," I say, breaking off the embrace. I can still hear the faint hum of Martha's car further down the street. "We're talking about trusting this woman with our pets and home."

I smile at Dan.

"And you know what?"

"What?"

"I do. I trust her."

CHAPTER THREE

I stay up late on Thursday night, cleaning the house before we leave on Friday morning. While I work, I get three texts from Martha, each one saying how excited she is about housesitting for the week and how she can't wait to spend time with Brogan and Billie. The texts are followed by a wall of emojis. Happy faces and love hearts. Puppies and kittens.

I reply to each one. Make a joke about the extensive notes I gave her and how I hope she's managing to squeeze in a life around reading them. She replies, saying she's studying them "diligently". That she probably knows Billie and Brogan better than I do by this point.

Being a night owl, it's not difficult for me to keep going. My headphones are on, and for the past hour I've been listening to a creative writing podcast. The episode I'm on is about motivation and the will to keep going when things feel hard or hopeless. It's a little corny, but it gives me a break from the true-crime podcasts that I've been bingeing on for the past few days in the car.

The bins go out. I change the bedsheets in our room,

which will be Martha's room for the next seven days. I wipe around the edge of the shower basin, mop the floors and vacuum the living room. Dan was out earlier in the day, tidying up the garden and driveway. Some trimming, some sweeping. Making sure things are presentable. I want Martha to be comfortable in our house and for the experience to be as pleasant as it possibly can be. If this Glencoe trip works out (fingers crossed), and we need another house sitter in the future, this might become a regular thing. We could even avoid going through the agency and work with Martha directly if she's interested. It would be great to use someone whom the pets are familiar with so they don't have to get used to a new face all the time. More work for her, more peace of mind for us.

It's a win-win.

Still, one step at a time. I don't want to get too ahead of myself, but I have a good feeling about this.

I get about four hours' sleep that night. Not bad, all things considered. I'm sure I'll sleep like a log when that Highland air hits me in Glencoe. Dan and I are both up with the birds, and Martha arrives on time later that morning, just as I hoped she would. Seven o'clock on the dot, it's a great start. Dan helps her inside with her suitcase.

"Welcome to your new home," he says, smiling.

Martha doubles over with laughter. I've already had a text from her this morning, telling me she was on her way. And then another one saying pretty much the same thing when she was sitting at a set of traffic lights. Lots of emojis and kisses, of course.

She notices our bags in the hallway, ready to be taken out and loaded into the car. Her eyes light up, and she rubs her palms together like she's trying to start a fire. To look at her, you'd think she was coming with us.

"Oooh! Are you two lovebirds excited about getting away from it all?"

I'm about to answer when there's a sound like stampeding horses from inside the house. Brogan thunders down the hallway, making a sudden appearance behind me. His tail wags at the sight of Martha. *Biscuit lady.* He's got one hell of a bark, which often scares people when they walk into the house for the first time. But he doesn't bark at Martha. Looks like he couldn't be happier to see her again. She leans over and gives him back rubs and offers him her hand to lick. She doesn't seem in the slightest bit concerned about getting hairs on her cardigan.

She's a dog person through and through, I think.

"You remember your auntie Martha," she says as he licks her face. The slobbering noises are both wet and loud. "Don't you, boy? Yes, you do. Don't you?"

"He sure does," I say.

"I ate a cookie in the car," Martha says. "I got caught at so many red lights that I started to get hungry. Had to raid the emergency stash, and I think Mr Brogan has found a little bit of sugar on my lips. Yes, you have, boy, haven't you? Have you found the sugar on Auntie Martha's lips?"

Brogan licks while Martha gives him kisses.

It's sweet.

It's also a little ... *much?*

Dan appears in the hallway, exchanges a few more pleasantries with Martha, then starts taking our bags out to the car. Here we go again – my heart is racing. This all happened so quickly, and now it's real. Now we've come to the moment where we walk out the door and leave the pets, and it's giving me a rush of light-headedness. It feels like the floor isn't quite there beneath me.

I follow Martha (and Brogan) into the kitchen and stand awkwardly in the doorway as she unloads some plastic containers from her bag and starts putting them into the fridge. I've made space for her by throwing out a heap of things Dan and I haven't used. By now, there are beads of sweat forming on my forehead. I check the dials on the oven, making sure everything is switched off. Then I do it again.

You can stay. Call it off. Dan will be furious, but he'll understand. We'll pay Martha the full fee plus a little more and apologise for the inconvenience. Money for nothing. She'll understand too.

"Excuse me, lovely."

Martha shuffles past me in the doorway, taking her bag into the living room. I follow like a puppy on her heels and watch as she sits down on the couch. She lets out a sigh like she's been on the go for days. Stretches her arms, then falls back into the couch. It's amazing how quickly she's making herself at home, yet I suppose she's used to this. It's the life of a house sitter, and it'll be an easier life if you can feel at home in someone else's house. It's good. She's comfortable here, and that can only be good news for the pets.

"You two just get yourselves ready," she says, glancing over her shoulder at me. She gives me a big smile, showing off her peg teeth. "Don't mind me." Brogan approaches and jumps on the couch, settling down beside her. Martha pulls my notes out of the front pocket of her bag and starts studying them while stroking Brogan's back with her free hand. Her tiny eyes narrow, as if labouring to see the words on the page. Is she doing this for my benefit? She did say in her texts last night that she'd studied them. *Diligently.* Why would she need to look at them now?

There are things in there she needs to know.

I walk further into the living room while Dan is still outside packing the car. I should be helping, but I can't bring myself to leave the house. The floor creaks under my weight. It feels like I'm creeping up on Martha as I approach the couch from the side. She doesn't look up, even when I'm standing right beside her.

I clear my throat.

"Everything okay?" I ask.

She looks up and gives me a wink. "All good, love."

Head down. She goes back to reading the notes and stroking the back of Brogan's neck. Humming softly under her breath.

"Excellent," I say. "Umm, can I just show you the pet door again? How it works, you know? Do you mind?"

She doesn't look up this time. "Hmm?"

"Do you mind if we just run through the pet door again? The latches can be a little tricky at first."

Finally, she looks up from the notes. The pause that follows lasts a lifetime.

"Yes. Of course, darling."

She stands up, and the sudden laugh she lets out is shrill enough to give me brain freeze. Martha puts the notes down on the couch, gives Brogan a pat and turns her full attention on me. We're standing facing one another, a little too close for comfort. I notice Martha's fruity-smelling perfume, and it's enough to make my nostrils twitch.

I smile. Take a step backwards and hope it's not too obvious.

"It'll just take a minute," I say.

She nods. "You show me again how the doggy door works."

"Okay."

I have no idea if I'm being annoying or not. What's that thing people do on Reddit – Am I the Asshole? Well, am I? Nonetheless, it's important that Martha figures this out. I don't want Brogan hitting his head on the door if she accidentally locks it from the outside when he's trying to get back in. And I don't want Billie Jean escaping after dark if it's not locked from the inside.

We have to get this right.

I kneel down and show Martha the settings. Once, twice, three times – I turn the latches slowly, demonstrating the multi-lock system and how to latch the door from the inside so no one can escape after hours. I think I'm explaining it clearly and concisely, but there's this blank look in her eyes. It's not sinking in. If she'd truly looked at the notes, which were accompanied by detailed photos, we wouldn't need to have this conversation.

Let it go. She'll figure it out.

"That's all there is to it," I say, standing back up and dusting down my jeans. I make sure there's enough space between us this time.

"Okay," she says. "I think I've got it now."

Fuck.

"Are you sure?"

"Yes."

There's a painful silence while I figure out what I'm going to say next. I either walk away and get on with the Glencoe holiday, or I press the matter.

"Can you show me, please?" I ask.

"What?"

"I'm sorry to be a pain; it's just so I know you've got it dialled in. I wouldn't want you to get confused later when you're on your own and you might not be able to reach us. I don't know what the phone signal will be like in some of the places we're going."

Martha looks at the pet door, then back at me. "You want me to show you?"

"Yes, please. Just lock it from the inside."

Another excruciating silence follows, broken only by the sound of a fly buzzing outside the window. Martha gives an exaggerated shrug, then kneels in front of the dog door. She groans on the way down, bothered by some joint or ligament pain that makes kneeling difficult. Her chubby fingers twirl the latches. Thirty seconds later, she stands up and lets out a raspy breath.

"Bad knees," she says. "Oh, it's no fun getting old, Angie love."

I'm looking at the pet door.

"That's not it."

"Hmm?"

"The door is still open. Brogan and Billie can still get out if they want to."

"Oh."

I kneel and turn the latches clockwise on both sides, locking the door from the inside. Alarm bells scream in my head.

"Oh righty," Martha says, looking down with a smile. "I see what you did there. Got it now."

I stand back up and dust down my jeans again. Despite what she says, I don't believe for a second that Martha has the door sussed. I sense the irritation working its way onto my face. I can no longer smile, and I'm about to ask her to show me again when the sound of floorboards creaking in the hallway tells me that Dan is back in the house. Sure enough, he walks into the living room. Oblivious to the tension, he's twirling the car key around his finger. Looking at me, a glint of excitement in his eyes.

"We all set?"

I don't answer.

Dan's laid-back smile wilts at the edges. "Everything okay?"

"Fine," Martha says. "Just getting to grips with this doggy door of yours. Those bloody latches, eh?"

"Right," Dan says, looking at the pet door and then at Martha. "It can be confusing at first, but you'll get it after a couple of tries."

"Absolutely. No one's worried here."

And just like that, all my concerns are shoved to the side. Who knows, maybe they're right, and maybe I am the asshole. I'm on edge, and even now, at the very last minute, I'm looking for ways to cancel the trip and just get on with my usual thing of being a basket case in mid-November. To stick with the familiar and safe.

Chill out. You heard what he said. She'll get it after a couple of tries.

Dan looks at me. Then he nods back towards the front door. "Guess we'd better hit the road while the traffic's a bit quieter. Ready to go?"

Those alarm bells are still ringing.

It feels like the moment has passed, though, and I can't ask Martha to show me again. *Think positive*, I tell myself. I'm just freaking out about leaving, and I know that Martha *will* figure it out after a while. It's not *that* hard. Not that complicated. Plus, she has instructions.

"All the bags are in the car?" I ask Dan.

"Everything's packed."

"Great."

Dan turns to Martha "Anything you need, just text or call."

"You bet," she says.

"Well then," I say, kneeling to unlock the pet door, "I guess we'd better go."

Martha follows us to the door while Brogan remains asleep on the couch. I've no idea where Billie Jean is. Probably off exploring somewhere, and I hope she doesn't disappear when she comes back and finds Martha in the house. We exchange brief goodbyes, and Dan is first out the door and down the driveway towards the car. Blue skies and autumnal sunshine will escort our exit out of the city. Perfect weather for travelling up to Loch Lomond today, and I know I should be so much more excited than this.

I stop in the doorway and look over my shoulder. Martha's standing in the hallway. She comes over and takes the edge of the door in her hand, watching me with that strange blankness in her tiny eyes.

It's not that hard, I remind myself. *She'll figure it out.*

I manage a feeble wave.

"Thanks again for doing this on such short notice."

"My pleasure, sweetie."

"Have fun," I say. "See you when we get back."

Martha waves me off as I walk towards the car. She calls after me in a high-pitched voice that rings in my ears. "Don't you worry," she says. "I'll take good care of things."

CHAPTER FOUR

Dan coughs as he grips the steering wheel, his knuckles unsheathing into sharp, white-tipped daggers.

"Bloody hell."

His attention jumps back and forth between me and the scenic winding road, his eyes probing for some hidden answer to the dilemma of a worsening cough.

"Are you okay?"

It's a stupid question. One I've asked several times over the past thirty hours or so since we set off on our broken-up journey to Glencoe. As Dan suggested, we've been taking it very slow, spending the first night in a lovely hotel at Loch Lomond and then scheduled for another tonight in an equally lovely hotel in Glen Etive. Breaking up a three-hour drive to the Laing house so that it takes us two days. That's my kind of pace, especially when there's so much to see. As for Dan, I think he just wants to go to Glen Etive because there's a famous James Bond movie location up there.

He shakes his head. "Feels like it's getting worse. My throat is inflamed."

"Stop the car for a second, will you?" I ask.

"What?"

"Just pull in up here to the left."

He pulls into a lay-by up ahead, then pauses the true-crime podcast that's been playing through the Bluetooth speakers.

Dan turns off the engine. Looks at me, the colour draining from his face.

"Talk to me, Ang. What do we do?"

I look outside at the picture-postcard scenery. It's classic Scottish shortbread-tin imagery. Blue skies, water and rugged mountains. The serenity outside is what we should be immersed in, not asking ourselves whether we should or shouldn't continue.

My phone pings.

"It's another text from Martha," I say, opening up the message.

"Another one?" Dan asks in a hoarse voice.

"Yup."

"How many texts has she sent since we left?"

"I stopped counting."

I show him the phone. It's Martha in the back garden with Billie and Brogan. She's lying on the grass, taking a selfie with the pets on either side of her. It's almost like they know they're having their photo taken and chose the perfect spot. They're both looking at the camera. It's one of many similar texts I've received since we set off. I guess I did ask for updates, but even I'll admit I wasn't expecting this many. Martha's sending everything to me even though she has Dan's mobile number as well.

"Well, at least they're having a good time," I say. "Looks like everything's going well back at the house."

Dan coughs. Then he slams the back of his skull against the headrest.

"Oh ... FUCK!"

He looks at me. Hope draining from his eyes.

"What do we do, Ang?"

IT'S SUPPOSED to be a fun trip, but I've been worried about Dan's worsening cough ever since we left Glasgow. He's tried to brave it out. Tried to ignore it. Tried to laugh it off. We both hoped that at some point it would go away or, at least, not get any worse. It's bad timing, that's all.

Awful timing.

The question is, do we keep going and see the trip through? We don't know if this is just a cold or something worse. Could be flu. Could be anything. Do we risk infecting the Laings and their partners? I'm not worried for myself because, if it's contagious, I'll get it anyway, considering the amount of time I've spent around Dan. But it's not right to go to someone else's house and make everyone else sick. That's not fair, no matter how much we need the break.

Despite Dan's cough, we've tried to make the best of the trip. The A82 connects the busy Central Belt to the Highlands, but more importantly it's an iconic stretch of road that passes by some of the most famous Scottish lochs and takes in more than its fair share of picturesque scenery as it winds its way north from Glasgow to Inverness.

On our first night, we're booked to stay in the stately Tarbet Hotel, right next to Loch Lomond. I'm still fairly relaxed at this point. It's tomorrow I'm worried about. Tomorrow is supposed to be a hiking day around Glen Etive.

That's not looking too promising. Dan's coughing, but it's not much worse than before, I suppose.

As for me, I'm feeling pretty good. I've put my anxieties about leaving the pets and the house down to perfectly normal concerns, amplified by a heightened state of stress because of Mum's anniversary.

Right now, I'm looking forward to a relaxing evening in the fancy hotel beside the loch. Doing nothing. The plan is to have a nice meal in the restaurant and a couple of drinks at the bar. Maybe enjoy a walk beside Loch Lomond at dusk and breathe in some of that fresh air. Just to enjoy it – that's what I want. To get away from the norm, distract myself from Mum's anniversary and do what she'd want me to do – get on with my life.

That's the plan.

But Dan's cough keeps getting worse.

We've checked into the hotel, and we're in the room, taking some things out of our cases. My phone chirps with more texts from Martha. It keeps pinging as she sends photos in individual clusters. Photos of the pets. Photos of herself in the kitchen, in the living room and in the garden. I mute my phone for a while so I can unpack my toiletries in peace. This is our one and only night in the Tarbet, and as much as I love the pets, I don't have to see photos of them every hour.

Still, I'm glad everyone's happy. And she means well.

"Do you want me to go down to reception and see if they've got any cough medicine?" I ask.

Dan's temporarily given up on the unpacking. He's standing at the window with its stunning view of Loch Lomond, Ben Lomond and the surrounding peaks. Although the hotel is located on the A82, it's quiet. I haven't heard a peep of traffic.

"Even if they do, it won't be much better than the stuff I've brought with me."

"You're sounding really hoarse. How do you feel?"

"Okay. Just feels like I'm starting to come down with something and ... well, what if I am? What happens to Glencoe if I'm ill?"

"I know," I say. "Can't really go up to the Laing house coughing and spluttering everywhere."

Dan sits down on the bed. He looks pale and miserable. With a sigh, he picks up his phone and slides his thumb over the screen in a distracted, mindless manner. I can tell he's trying not to think about the possibility of cancelling the holiday. But the fear of exactly that is written all over his face.

"We'll see how it looks tomorrow," he says. "I'm sure it'll be fine. I probably just need a good night's sleep."

As if to convince me, he gets up off the bed with a spring in his step and continues unpacking. He hangs up one of his good shirts in the wardrobe. The one he's planning to wear to dinner, and now he's debating out loud whether to iron it or not. If he does, it'll be the first non-work item of clothing that he's ironed in years. He goes to the bathroom and comes out with a toothbrush hanging out of his mouth like a cigarette.

My phone pings again.

Dan frowns. "Let me guess. Martha?"

I nod. "She's keen. Maybe she just thinks it's part of her job to send constant updates. Like on the hour every hour."

"I thought your phone was on mute."

I smile. "I lasted about five minutes. You know, if there's an emergency ..."

Dan's forehead wrinkles as he slips another shirt over a coat hanger. He hangs it up, then closes the wardrobe door.

He walks over, his eyes locked on the phone in my hand. "She does have my number too, doesn't she?"

"Yep. I gave her both."

"Why isn't she sending me any updates?"

"Maybe she thinks it's easier to have one contact. I don't know."

Dan coughs. Looks at his watch. "It's after five o'clock now. Maybe the updates will stop for the rest of the night."

"She's harmless," I say. "It must be hard going into someone else's house, knowing that you're responsible for their pets. She just wants to reassure me they're okay. Probably because I kept pushing about the pet door."

After we left the house on Friday, I told Dan all about what happened with Martha and the pet door. How she didn't have a clue about working the latches and how it was freaking me out for a while there. Imagining the possibilities. Envisioning disaster. He reassured me that she'd figure it out, and I've been able to accept it. And as we travelled north on the A82, the gnawing doubt I felt about our decision to leave the house began to settle.

Dan gestures towards the window and the magnificent view. "Want to go for a walk before dinner?"

"Does your *cough* want to go for a walk before dinner?"

"Only one way to find out."

WE GO for a walk and don't hear from Martha while we're outside. I don't think too much about the fact she's sending me all those texts. Sending? Bombarding? It's a bit much, but right now we've got bigger things to worry about. Like, is Dan fit to go on holiday? And if we're going to turn back and return to Glasgow, isn't it better to do it before we drive another fifty miles north to Glencoe?

The problem is, I know what Dan's like. He'll take this to the wire. I also know how much he wants to see his old friends. He probably feels some pressure to see it through for me too, because of the whole Mum thing. It was his idea after all. And Dan needs it too. It must be exhausting walking on eggshells around me at this time of year. The slightest little thing can set me off, and to put it mildly, I'm a gigantic pain in the arse. I know this. I hate what I become in November.

We walk along a nice gravel track beside the loch, under a pink and orange sky that reflects off the surface of the water. Dan keeps coughing. I don't make a big deal of it, but the conversation is stilted. Dan tries a little small talk as we make our way back to the hotel, but he's still coughing at dinner too. His eyes are watering with frustration as he tries to hold them in. He persuades me not to fuss even though I'm ready to call an end to the holiday right there.

"I know what you're thinking," he says.

"And?"

"I'll be fine."

"Will you?"

"I will," Dan says, lowering his spoon into a bowl of soup.

"Dan, it's okay if we reschedule this thing. Health comes first, and at the end of the day, the Laings will understand."

"Let's just check in tomorrow morning," Dan says. He forces a smile across the dinner table. "Then we'll see where we're at."

"I know what you're like," I say. "You'll push through,

but it's not just about us. It's about the people we don't want to pass anything on to. Remember?"

He's halfway through sipping his wine. Acting like he's not listening. "Hmm?"

"You heard me. Are you really up for a twelve-hour hike tomorrow?"

"Easy, tiger. I'll feel great after a good night's sleep."

I hear myself pushing and back off. Instead, I finish the wine that's left in my glass. Pour myself another because, why not? As of this moment, I'm still on holiday. No point in wasting a perfectly good bottle of wine, and who knows? This might be the highlight of a very short trip. We sit in silence while I tap my fingers on the edge of the table. The classical music that plays softly in the restaurant is like a wasp buzzing in my ears.

My phone vibrates in my pocket.

Dan hears the buzz. He arches his eyebrows. "Surely that's not her?"

"It's her," I say, pulling out my phone. Dan shakes his head and continues to drink his wine while I open up the message.

"More photos," I say. "Billie, Brogan and Martha. And *lots* of emojis."

"Looks like you two are best pals now."

"Who?"

"You and Martha."

"Looks like it."

Dan holds his wine glass by the stem, pinching it with his thumb, index and middle fingers. He looks like a professional wine taster.

"She loves you."

"Well," I say with a wicked grin, "I am very loveable.

And to be honest – I don't care how many texts and photos she sends as long as she's taking good care of my pets. Why does she always have to send so many close-ups of herself though?"

"It's because she loves—"

Dan explodes into a sudden coughing fit. It's a big one. We get a few worried looks from diners at the other tables, who probably think there's someone choking to death and ruining their nice meal. They quickly look away, and I get the feeling that if Dan *was* choking to death, they wouldn't rush to his assistance.

I wait until he's gotten it under control. But his face is red and flushed.

"Dan, we made a mistake."

"It's fine," he says. He takes a sip of water and looks around the restaurant as if to apologise for the disturbance. "Please, Ang, stop fussing. Let's wait until tomorrow before we make any big decisions."

NOW HERE WE ARE, parked in the lay-by. The road is quiet, and there's no sign of any other traffic. For now at least, it's like we have the Highlands to ourselves.

Of course, Dan woke up in the morning and said he was feeling much better. And he wasn't coughing quite as badly as he had been the night before. Still, it was a rough night. He said he was okay to keep going, and I rolled with it for the sake of peace. He even said the hike around Glen Etive would do him good.

"What do we do?" he asks.

My stomach clenches into a tight knot. As far as I'm

concerned, the decision has already been made even if neither one of us has said it out loud yet. The very fact that he's now asking tells me everything. But Dan isn't going to be the one to say it. For whatever reason, he needs to hear it from me.

"I think the holiday is over, Dan. I think we need to go home and take care of you."

I lower the phone onto my lap. I've turned the sound and vibration mode off, so I don't have to deal with any more Martha texts. I appreciate her keeping us in the loop, but I need a little space from that right now.

"I'm sorry," Dan says.

"What do you mean?"

"This was for you. I wanted to get you away from the norm for a while. See if it helped."

"Next year," I say. "And hey, I think you're right about us taking a break in mid-November. Let's do it. Let's make it a thing from next year on. Maybe we'll come back here if the Laings are up in November."

"I'd like that," Dan says. He talks in a raspy, painful-sounding voice.

I blow him a kiss. He catches it with a smile.

"Oh well," I say, picking up my phone, "I'd better let Martha know we're coming back."

"I wonder how she'll take it."

"She'll understand."

I call Martha. It goes straight to voicemail.

"I'll text her," I say. "Oh, no, sod it. She'll probably just send me more photos if I start communicating. Let's go back and tell her in person. We owe her that much. We'll apologise and explain that she's getting the full fee. And a glowing five-star review – written by you."

Dan nods. "That's fair."

"More than fair."

"Judging by those photos," Dan says, "Billie and Brogan will be devastated we've come back early. Looks like they're having fun with their auntie Martha."

"They'll forgive us."

Dan flops back into the driver's seat with a disappointed sigh. He doesn't have to try to pretend that everything's alright anymore. I think he saw the writing on the wall for this trip as soon as the cough started getting worse. We both did. It sucks because we've been in a rut lately, and our daily routines have taken us away from each other more than we'd like. My delivery job, which keeps me out all night, doesn't help. A full week off work and a normal holiday routine would've been so good for us. But life has other plans.

I drop the phone onto my lap, and for a few minutes we both sit in silence, staring out towards the vast cluster of hills beyond the loch. Misty clouds descend from the heavens, veiling the top of the hills. What little sunlight we had is gone.

Dan looks longingly at the road ahead, and I think, in his mind, he can see all the way to Glencoe. All the way to the Laing mansion. It's a vision that's slipping out of reach. "You're absolutely sure about this?"

I nod. "Yes."

He coughs, and I give him a gentle pat on the shoulder.

"Dan," I say, "let's go home."

CHAPTER FIVE

I take the wheel and drive us back down the A82 to Glasgow.

It's official. The holiday to Glencoe has been abandoned, and more than anything else, I'm gutted for Dan, who's quiet on the way back. Very quiet. At first, I think he's sleeping on the journey home. His head is pressed up against the window, and he's using his jacket as a pillow. But his eyes are open. He's watching the scenery go by.

I make a few feeble attempts at conversation. It doesn't go anywhere.

The only thing that matters now is getting back and taking care of Dan. I just want to get him home, but I need to be careful. The A82 is beautiful, but alongside its spectacular scenery, it has a reputation as being one of the most dangerous stretches of road in Britain. There are many sudden twists and turns, and I have to concentrate on what's in front of me. Won't be hard considering there's so little to say right now. I don't even put on a podcast or any music. We travel in silence.

Less than two hours later, we're pulling up in the driveway behind Martha's silver Corsa. We haven't called or texted since those initial attempts to get in touch with her. Doing it over the phone or via text doesn't feel right. This is something we have to do face to face, and besides, it's a legitimate reason for coming back early. Dan is ill with the flu or something, and we can't be so selfish as to spread it up there in Glencoe.

Martha's a nice person. She might be disappointed, but she'll understand.

We leave the cases and the rest of our things in the boot.

Dan and I trudge up the driveway, exchanging tense looks. It's strange to feel this nervous about coming back home. Dan's looking pale, and as soon as Martha's gone, I'll put fresh sheets on the bed and send him in there to sleep. Meanwhile, I'll go out and stock up on some cold and flu treatment. Do a food shop. Then I'll book him a doctor's appointment for Monday morning. Not quite the weekend I was expecting to have.

"You'll be fine," I say, as we walk to the door.

Dan nods. He's still putting on a brave face for my sake. When we're both up to it, we can start making plans for another trip. Maybe back up to Glencoe. Maybe we'll go overseas somewhere. No more short-notice getaways, though – they're far too stressful.

"Do we knock?" he asks, when we reach the door.

I snatch the keys out of his hand.

"We live here."

"I know, but we should probably knock. Manners."

"Fine."

I knock, and we wait, but there's no answer. There's a doorbell, but it hasn't worked since we first moved in, and neither one of us has ever bothered to report it to the landlord. I can hear the TV blaring in the living room, and it's loud enough that Brogan hasn't started barking, which he almost always does when there's a knock on the door.

"I tried," I say to Dan. With that, I insert the key into the lock. "It's okay. She'll understand."

Dan doesn't have the energy to argue. He looks like he's in the trenches, waiting for the signal to go over the top. His voice is croaky and tired. "Agreed. Let's go in."

I open the door, and the TV skyrockets in volume. She needs it *that* loud? Sounds like she's watching one of those generic daytime quiz shows, aka brain rot, and right now it's loud enough to make one's ears bleed. We creep into our own home like burglars, and it's when I glance into the kitchen from the hallway that I get the first big slap in the face. It looks like a bomb has gone off in there. Dirty dishes are piled sky-high in the sink, and now that Dan's closed the door behind us, I gag on a rotten, fruity stench. It's like smelling the inside of a bin that's been left out on a hot day.

I look at Dan. He silently mouths back to me: "What the fuck?"

"She hasn't even been here two full days," I say.

This is not what I was expecting. Is this why all the photos that Martha sent were close-ups of her and the pets? Was she trying to hide the state of the house in the background?

She still hasn't heard us over the sound of the TV.

"Where's Brogan?" I ask, my heart smashing against my ribs. "Why isn't he running to the door to meet us?"

Dan touches his ear. Then he gestures to the living-room door; it's closed. "He can't hear us over that crappy game show or whatever it is."

My arms go taut with tension.

"Let's get in there," I say, pointing to the door.

There's a surge of panic, and it comes on so strong that I fight the urge to be sick. Where's my dog? Where's my cat? I barge past Dan, blocking out the sight of all those dirty cups, glasses and plates left to rot in the kitchen. We have a dishwasher! Why doesn't she put them in there and start the damn thing? I can't block it all out. And I see there are used takeaway cartons on the floor, too. Two days – not even two days in the house – and Martha has turned our sanctuary into a dump.

She's a slob.

We rushed. We made a mistake.

Get her out.

I don't knock this time. I thunder across the hallway and pull the door open. I'm not sure who screams first. Me or her.

Martha is lying on her back on the couch, feet propped up on the armrest. She is stark naked. She screams again as I stand horrified at the living-room door. My body frozen. I'm paralysed for about ten seconds. I can't move. Then she leaps up off the couch with the sort of athleticism that only the most sudden of shocks can instil in a non-athletic body. She crosses her arms over her breasts. Bends over, becoming a hunchback to hide her top half. Legs pressed tight together, trying to conceal her private parts. Her arms are covered in faded tattoos, something I hadn't expected to see on quirky cosy Martha. She kneels and grabs her dressing gown, which is a scrunched-up pink heap on the floor. She covers herself up. Her face is beetroot red as her shrill voice wails over the TV.

"What are you doing?"

I can't speak. I can hardly breathe. The living room is in

the same state as the kitchen. There's a giant bowl on the coffee table, smeared around the edges with something that looks like vanilla ice cream. There are empty crisp packets on the floor. I count five of them. Chocolate wrappers too. There's a bottle of wine on the table, next to the ice-cream bowl, and a glass that's tipped over. Next to the table on the carpet, a blotchy red puddle. Is that a wine stain?

She's trembling. Her entire body is trembling as her top half rocks back and forth. Her shoulders twitch. She doesn't even look at Dan. She's looking at me. Her words are addressed to me and me only, so it seems.

"Why did you come back?"

Neither Dan nor I have spoken since walking into the living room. Not a single word has come out of either one of us. I feel like I've been punched in the face, and now the inside of my head is like a pinball machine. My thoughts slamming off the walls of my mind.

"What's going on?" Martha asks, clutching the edge of her dressing gown. "Say something, for God's sake."

But I can't. I'm still taking it all in. And now I notice something that looks like a puddle of vomit on the floor next to the armchair where Brogan likes to sleep. The sight of it tightens a cold, hard knot in my stomach.

Martha's mumbling to herself. Digging her fingernails into the skin of her forearm, pulling up the sleeve of her dressing gown as she rakes at her flesh. One of the tattoos leaps out at me. It's huge. Looks like a bear or maybe a dog's head. The ink is too dull and smudgy to be sure.

She stops scratching. Pulls the sleeve down, covering the tattoo.

"Well?" she asks. "What's going on?"

Finally, I find my voice.

I step further into the shithole that used to be our living room.

"Where's Brogan and Billie Jean?" I ask in a shaky voice. "Where are my pets, Martha?"

Her face wrinkles with confusion. She blinks fast. Looks from one end of the room to another in surprise, as if to imply that Billie and Brogan were curled up at her feet just seconds ago.

I glare at her. "Well?"

Her bottom lip trembles. "They ... they're ... in the back garden."

I point to the window that looks out onto the back of the house. "They're outside?"

"Yes."

I march over, grab the remote control off the couch and turn off the TV. The sudden silence inside the house is jarring. But it doesn't last long. My footsteps sound like mini explosions as I charge over to the window, pull back the blinds and look outside.

"Thank God," I whisper.

Brogan is oblivious to the chaos unfolding inside the house. He's plodding about, sniffing the flower beds over at the back fence. Meanwhile, Billie Jean is napping on the old sun recliner that's covered in cobwebs. If she can hear anything, it's not getting in the way of her nap.

I look back at Dan.

"They're okay."

He nods but still can't talk.

I suck in a deep lungful of air and take a step back from the window. Before that, I pull the blinds open further to shine a light on the mess in the living room. My body feels like it's vibrating from head to toe. I glance at the pet door near my feet. The latches are in the proper daytime position. Well, at least she figured those out even if the rest of the house is a disaster zone.

I blink away the white dots in front of my eyes.

She's standing in the middle of the room, still clutching the edges of her dressing gown tightly together. Looking at me like I'm crazy. And she's still paying no attention to Dan.

"Of course they're okay," she says. "What did you think? That I would let something happen to them?"

I glance over at Dan still hovering at the doorway. This is the last thing he needed, and it looks like he's about to pass out.

"What the hell, Martha? Look at this place."

Martha's dot eyes narrow to the point of disappearing. Slowly, she takes off her glasses, and the way she looks at me, her eyes unveiled, turns my blood to ice. She speaks, and I've never heard her voice so quiet.

"What did you say?"

My jaw tightens, and I resist the urge to throw water over this fire. To back off, even to apologise for barging in like we did.

"Look at the state of the place," I say. "There's puke on the carpet and a wine stain on the floor. Why was Brogan sick? Why haven't you cleaned it up? This isn't what I expected of a professional house sitter, Martha."

Martha keeps her eyes on me. "You hired me."

"And we made a mistake," I say. "That much is obvious."

She puts her glasses back on and has a look around the room. The look on her face is ... *bored*. "It's just a bit of mess. I was going to tidy everything up."

"A bit of mess?"

"Why are you back?" she asks. The way she's talking, it's

like I've done something wrong. Like I'm the one who's violated her sacred space. "Why are you talking to me like this, Angie darling? I thought we were friends."

I feel like I've been pushed.

"Friends? Martha, we're paying you to be here. Paying you to look after the house and the pets."

I'm about to tell her to pack her things when something else catches my eye. Two bowls of kibble on the floor at the far end of the couch, close to the pet door. There's a mixture of dog and cat food in each bowl. Both bowls are spilling over with food.

My finger stabs in that direction.

"What's that? We don't leave food lying around – I wrote that down, and I told you as well, remember? Brogan's a gorger. He'll eat himself sick. I guess that's what happened, eh? And why is there cat AND dog food in the same bowl?"

My voice is spiralling towards a hysterical shriek. Every time I start to calm down, I see something else that makes it even worse. This is a nightmare. Am I still tucked up in bed in the hotel in Loch Lomond?

"I was going to clean up," Martha says. "You should have told me you were coming back."

I shake my head. "That's not the point, and even if it were, we called and got your voicemail. Quite frankly, Martha, I'm glad you didn't pick up. Otherwise, I might never have known what sort of house sitter you are."

The smell of rotten food, puke and rubbish is making me queasy. The woman we brought in to look after the place has turned our home into a landfill dump. It's beyond unacceptable. What's really pissing me off, however, is that Martha doesn't seem to understand the problem. She hasn't apologised. She seems more interested in finding out why we're back early rather than focusing on the damage she's caused.

She folds her arms. "I'm booked here for a week."

"Martha," I say, "I wouldn't leave you in my house for another hour. Please pack your things and go. I don't know if we can get our deposit back from the agency, but we sure as hell won't be paying the full sum for this. I'll be telling them as much."

She blinks hard again. Her upper lip curls ever so subtly into something that looks like a snarl. "Are you going to complain about me?"

I sweep my hand in a theatrical gesture across the living room.

"Look around you. Damn right I'm going to complain."

Martha takes a step towards me. My vision of the fluffy cardigan woman is long gone, and I don't know who *this* person is. Her fists are clenched at the sides. At that moment, I feel the ancient evolutionary forces stirring deep inside me. It's fight or flight.

"Don't," she says.

"Don't?"

"I need my job."

"Well, you should've thought of that, shouldn't you? And actually done your job properly."

"Okay – that's enough."

It's Dan who hurriedly positions himself in between us. The gesture isn't subtle, and he holds his arms out to separate us like a boxing referee. "Martha – it's time you left. Please pack your suitcase and go. This obviously isn't working."

The sound of Dan's voice brings Martha back from the brink of whatever abyss she was standing over. She looks at Dan like he materialised out of thin air. Then her eyes well up, and she hurries past us, waddling at high speed out of the living room. Dan and I stay put. Listening to her crying as she gets dressed and packs her things.

I can't stop shaking. My heart is thumping.

"Oh shit," Dan whispers. His bulging eyes are the epitome of *what the fuck just happened*.

I have no answer to that question, at least not yet. I knew our sudden return would be awkward, but I never dreamed for one second that we were walking into something like this. I trusted her. I trusted Martha, and I got it wrong.

Five long minutes pass. Martha storms down the hallway with her bags like a charging rhinoceros. The door opens. She leaves without saying another word and slams the door shut like she's trying to blow it off the hinges.

"Oh shit," I say. "We're parked behind her."

"I'll go," Dan says quickly. "Otherwise she might ram into us."

While he's outside, I'm alone in the house. And despite what just took place, whatever the hell that was, I feel better for it. Or at least I'll feel better once I've cleaned every last trace of Martha Hunt out of my home.

It's done. Lesson learned about short-notice house sitters.

The main thing is she's gone. And, thank God, I'll never have to see her again.

CHAPTER SIX

"Dan!"

I yell from the bedroom to the living room, where Dan's spread out on the couch, watching the second season of *Succession*. It's his latest viewing obsession, and I think, so far today, that he's devoured three episodes without so much as moving. I call to him again, and this time, the volume is lowered.

"What's up?" he calls to me.

"Have you seen my photo album?"

"The what?"

I raise my voice. "My photo album. *The* photo album."

"Haven't seen it."

"Are you sure?"

"Sure. Don't you keep it in your top drawer?"

"That's where it's supposed to be," I say. I'm looking into that same drawer as I talk to him. The top drawer where I keep my socks and underwear. The photo album is meant to be buried underneath a shallow pile of clothes. It's always there. Except today. Today, there's nothing there but my socks and undies.

This is not good.

That photo album is my last worldly connection to Mum. That means it's priceless. The photos that I've pasted inside the album are all the images of Mum that exist in the world. I'm pretty sure there are no others. I've got a few black-and-white pictures of her as a child, and there's one in particular that I love where she's standing in the garden of her childhood home, holding a little antique parasol over her head. There's a slightly worried look on her face. Sometimes I look at the photo and wonder if she knew the world was going to be too much for her.

There are photos of Mum as a teenager and as an adult when she developed her fondness for sixties-era hair and fashion. Her extended Brigitte Bardot phase, as she liked to call it, which was something that never went away. It's a small album, and there are other things in there that have meaning, besides the small collection of photographs. There are old writing assignments that I did for therapy classes. Things I wrote about Mum that no one else, not even my aunt Rose or uncle Matt, and not even Dan later on, was ever supposed to read. That's when I discovered the healing power in writing. In pouring out my thoughts and feelings, unfiltered onto the page with brutal honesty. It wasn't easy, but it was rewarding, and I kept those pages because they were essentially *me* on the page. Messed up but hanging in there. A good summation of my life so far.

The album is everything. It's what keeps Mum alive.

It *never* leaves this room.

I must be getting forgetful lately, because I've forgotten to lock the door twice when I was going out over the past week. That's not like me. Makes me wonder if I'm still hung up on the mid-November crazies. Even though we're past the date itself. Even though it should be getting easier.

I wanted to look through the album because I've decided to attend an open therapy session at the university tonight. It'll be my first session in nearly two years. I want to check in and maybe talk, maybe just listen to others as they work through their own problems. That environment works for me sometimes. I don't know what it is, but it's like a rope pulling me back up to the light. Tonight's session at Strathclyde University is open to any kind of lingering trauma, and it can be something that happened recently or, as in my case, something that's lingered for decades. Maybe I'll start going back on a regular basis again. Maybe not, but I wanted to go through the album before heading out tonight. Looking at it always brings Mum closer, and that helps if I'm going to talk about her to a roomful of strangers. I was even thinking about taking it with me and browsing through it on the train. Particularly some of the things I wrote about her when I was younger. The memories come easier that way, with the images and words in front of me.

I was so young at the time. My biggest fear now is forgetting her.

The TV goes quiet in the living room. The hallway floorboards make their spectacularly over-the-top creaking noise, which means Dan is up on his feet and, most likely, on his way to the bedroom. Sure enough, he pokes his head through the open doorway. His smile fizzles out when he sees the expression on my face.

"Hey. Are you okay?"

I shake my head. "Dan, where could it be?"

"It's okay. It's here somewhere."

"Where?" I ask. "Did I do something stupid that I can't remember?"

"Like what? And why would you do something stupid with the album?"

"Because it's November."

Dan shakes his head. "No. It's been better this year, don't you think?"

"Dan, I've left the front door unlocked twice this week. That's not like me. I feel like my mind is playing cruel tricks on me."

"It's okay. It happens."

"It feels like November fifteenth is sticking around a little longer this year. Still casting its spell. Still messing with me."

I look at him.

"Are you sure you didn't move it?"

His expression is so sincere that I feel bad for even thinking to ask the question. I'm grateful he doesn't use it to start an argument.

"I'd never touch your mum's photo album, you know that. And if for some reason I had to, I'd guard it with my life. I know what it means to you."

"I know," I say, nodding. "I'm sorry."

He walks into the bedroom. We stand shoulder to shoulder, looking into the top drawer where the album should be.

"You definitely haven't moved it?" he asks.

"No."

He clicks his fingers. "What about before we left to go to Glencoe? You were doing a lot of cleaning. Maybe you ... I don't know ... maybe you picked it up and put it down somewhere? It's probably in the cupboard there, right?"

I shake my head. "This drawer is where I always leave it.

Underneath the pile of underwear and socks – it's always buried right *there*. If I take it out, I always put it back. Always. It's the one thing that never leaves this room or goes anywhere else."

Dan nods. "Okay."

"And yet," I say, "it's missing. It's not there."

"So where could it be?"

I don't answer. Instead, I glance at my watch.

"Still going to the session tonight?" Dan asks.

"Yep."

"Okay."

"I'd better have a shower," I say, closing the drawer. "I've got a train to catch."

My phone pings on the bed. I turn around, pick it up and look at the text message on the home screen.

"Fuck."

"She's still texting you?" Dan asks.

I nod while deleting Martha's text. "She truly thought we were friends. *Friends.* Can you believe that? She's still apologising for what she did, begging for forgiveness. She even wants to meet up and talk. Look at all these emojis. Love hearts. Does she think she's fourteen or something?"

"Maybe it's time to block her."

"I did that. This is a different number she's calling from. It's like she got another phone just to keep sending me these apology texts."

We exchange looks of bewilderment.

"Ignore her," Dan says. "She'll give up sooner or later."

IT'S BEEN ten days since the Martha disaster. That's the official title that Dan and I have given it.

I made a formal complaint to the agency. There was no way I could just let it go, not after the way she conned me into thinking everything was hunky-dory and happy-clappy at home with all those photos of her and the pets. Dan wanted me to let it go. He thought there could be something wrong with Martha, some sort of mental disability that we should be considerate of. I told him that was bullshit. But that's Dan. He's too nice for his own good. Martha's "disability" is that she's a shit house sitter. A million apology texts weren't going to save her. She wrecked our house. She risked the health and safety of our pets.

While I was cleaning the house that day we came back, I found more dog vomit under our bed. Hard and crusty on the carpet. Like it had been clotting there for days. It gives me nightmares to think about what might have happened to Billie Jean and Brogan if we'd been gone for a full week.

The train pulls out of the station. I sit down at one of the table seats and lean my head against the window. As we pick up speed, a woman's voice comes through the speakers to inform passengers that the next and final stop is Glasgow Queen Street.

I look at the empty table in front of me.

Something's missing. It's the photo album. It should be here, and it's gone.

Missing, not gone.

Did I put it in one of the suitcases so I could take it to Glencoe with me? Or did I move it with the intention of putting it in one of the suitcases?

No. It never leaves the bedroom.

I complained about Martha's shabby housesitting by

phone and then, at the request of the agency management, sent more details by email. Those follow-up details were accompanied by a *lot* of photos: puddles of dog vomit, the carnage she left in the kitchen and living room, and one close-up of a leftover box of white rice with two cockroaches having a party in it. The agency rep I spoke to was hugely apologetic. What else could she do? She refunded our deposit, and the last thing she said before we ended the call was that she'd "take care of the situation" and "ensure it would never happen again".

I had an idea of what that meant.

Then again, Martha was sending all those apology texts, so maybe she wasn't taken off their books. Maybe apologising was something the agency requested that she do, and Martha went a bit overboard.

I don't know what happened to Martha. I don't care. It's done. Having said that, I'd be amazed if she's still on their books as a potential house sitter after all the info and evidence I sent through. It taught me a lesson: never allow a complete stranger to look after my pets and house. Short-notice holidays aren't an option. And even if it's planned long in advance, we don't go anywhere until we find someone we trust.

New rules.

The train is quiet as it speeds towards Glasgow city centre. No surprise, I guess. It's midweek, and there aren't a lot of people heading into town. Most of the commuters will have come and gone by now. I find the photo of Mum on my phone, but it's not the same as having the photo album laid out in front of me. That's kind of a ritual. Turning the pages, looking at her face again. Doing that, I remember her voice. The way she walked. The way she liked to sing sometimes.

From Queen Street, it's a ten-minute walk to the university building where the session is being held. I'm one of the last to arrive. I don't know anyone in the session, which is led by a fifty-something woman called Belinda, who speaks with a strong Belfast accent.

Here I am again. Different place, different faces, but it's the same old thing. That's okay – it's what I need right now to settle my mind. We do the rounds, and in the end, I do talk for a few minutes. I talk about what happened to Mum, and that always gets people to pay attention. The same old phrases pop up about moving on and healing and closure. It's predictable but comforting. Like a favourite film that I've seen dozens of times but keep revisiting. I also mention that I'm kind of forgetful at the moment. Forgetting to lock the door. Misplacing the photo album. Everyone nods, and their understanding makes me feel better.

"That was very brave of you," Belinda says, approaching me after the session. She lets out a quiet breath. I noticed during the session that she likes a long pause before speaking. "You've been through a lot."

I smile. "Thanks."

"This wasn't your first session tonight, was it?"

I shake my head. "It's been a while. I've been on and off over the years. Open sessions here at the uni and all over Glasgow."

"Let me guess. November, mostly?"

"Yep. Always around the anniversary."

She gives me a pat on the shoulder. "You're doing well, Angie. You're doing *brilliantly*."

"Thanks."

"Come back anytime," Belinda says. "You're always welcome."

I don't hang around for long. Some of the others have gathered at the table for tea, coffee and biscuits. Belinda walks over to join them. Sometimes it's nice to stick around and chat, but I don't feel like staying. I came here tonight to feel it out and be a "beginner" again. That's enough for this week.

I say a brief goodbye to Belinda and the others. Then I walk outside into the cool night. There's a smell in the air that reminds me of candy floss. People walk up and down the city streets, wrapped up in big coats like it's the heart of winter. It feels mild to me, and the cold air is especially welcome after the session, where Belinda had the radiators on full blast, and the room felt like a furnace.

I'm in no hurry as I walk back towards the train station. It's been a while since I've been in the city centre, so I slow down and take in the surroundings. The intricacies of Glaswegian architecture entertain me as I stroll along – the statues and sculptures that peek out over the city streets. It's important to look up in Glasgow because you never know what's looking down at you.

I cross the road, making my way onto George Square and heading north towards the station. It's busier than I expected it to be. The Christmas lights have been switched on to mark the beginning of the festive season, and I suppose that might have a little something to do with the hustle and bustle. Still, it's not full-on yet. The market will be up and running soon, and there'll be fairground-style rides and a skating rink. That's when it's going to be full-on festive season. Maybe I'll persuade Dan to go ice-skating with me. That should be funny, considering he couldn't stay on his feet for more than ten seconds the last time we went.

I walk past the war memorial. Then I stop.

The hairs on the back of my neck are standing up. At the same time, the city noise recedes into the background, and I become aware of something else. Footsteps. Someone is behind me. Closing the gap.

Nothing unusual about someone walking behind me in the city centre.

So why did I stop?

I start walking again, and there it is. Loud footfalls in my ear – *thump-thump-thump*. Whoever it is, they're right behind me. It's a matter of inches, and I wonder if that's the breeze on the back of my neck or someone's breath.

There's no mistaking this feeling.

Someone is following me.

CHAPTER SEVEN

You're being ridiculous.

George Square is full of people. Of course I can hear the sound of footsteps behind me. I'm in Glasgow city centre, and even though the Christmas festivities haven't begun in earnest, there are still plenty of people around. Feels like it's getting busier as the night goes on.

I've stopped again. I'm still beside the famous war memorial on the eastern side of the square. The two sculptured lions that form part of the memorial are silent witnesses to the relentless back and forth of locals and tourists.

I continue on my way towards the train station. I haven't taken five steps before something hits me from behind. *Rams* me. Feels like one of those stone lions has pounced on me as soon as I showed them my back. I'm knocked off my feet and fall forward, getting my arms out just in time to stop myself faceplanting on the ground.

What the hell?

Did someone just shove me from behind?

I jump back to my feet without thinking. There's already a small crowd gathering around me, and it feels like they've come out of nowhere. I hear voices asking if I'm okay. One guy with a grey suit on has got a hold of my arm like he thinks I'm a drunk who'll topple over if he lets go. All these things are in the background for me. My senses continue to circle the airport, waiting to land.

"Who did it?" I blurt out.

My eyes scour the people in George Square. Most of them continue on their way, a few occasional glances in the direction of the small crowd that's clustered around me.

"Are you okay?" a young woman with a backpack on asks. Her accent sounds Swedish.

"I'm fine."

"Did you fall?" the man in the suit asks.

"Fall? I was pushed. Didn't you—?"

"You were pushed?" the Swedish woman asks.

"Didn't you see? Didn't anyone see who did it?"

She shakes her head. "Sorry. You were already down by the time I got over here."

"Same here," says the man.

I check my hands for cuts and scrapes. "Someone pushed me in the back."

I hear a sudden explosion of laughter from one of the nearby pubs on the outskirts of George Square. Two men in a doorway, smoking and sharing jokes. It's a world away from this confusing moment.

"Someone shoved me from behind," I say again.

The crowd around me starts to thin. Those on the outskirts of the huddle slip away now that the action is over.

"It was probably an accident," the Swedish woman says. She's inching away too. "You're okay?"

I give her a weak nod. Then I dust the front of my coat down.

"Fine."

There's some nervous laughter among those who're left. A "joke" from someone about me having one too many drinks. I'd get mad if I were paying much attention.

Was it an accident? Just some halfwit rushing across the square and paying no attention to whom they bumped into? Not even stopping to apologise? There's certainly enough of them in the world.

"I'd better be going," I say.

I check to make sure nothing has fallen out of my pocket. Someone has already handed me my bag, and when I pat my jeans, my phone is still there. Whatever happened, it definitely wasn't an attempt to steal anything.

I mumble a brief thanks to those who stuck around to make sure I was okay.

Then I hurry towards the train station.

CHAPTER EIGHT

I don't tell Dan what happened.
    The shove or fall (if you believe the onlookers) was horrible. I couldn't stop thinking about it on the train back home and almost missed my stop as a result. No matter how many times I replay that moment in my mind, it doesn't ever feel like someone bumping into me by accident.
    It was deliberate.
    It was definitely deliberate.
    I know I should tell Dan, but I can't bring myself to do it. So when I get home, I kiss him on the cheek, pour myself a glass of wine and veg out on the couch to watch TV with him. He's watching some dystopian series about a major city that's been walled off from the rest of the world after a bunch of riots. Billie Jean and Brogan are curled up on the couch beside us. I stroke Brogan's back while he snores. And while he does that, I replay the shove for the thousandth time in my mind.
    "Glad you went?" Dan asks.
    "Hmm?"

"To the session tonight. Glad you went?"

I nod. "Yeah."

I pick up the remote before Dan can ask me any more questions about the session. I'm not in the mood to talk.

I KEEP BUSY. Writing by day, delivering food by night. That's all my life is, so I roll with the punches and try to put the missing photo album and the George Square incident behind me.

This morning, I'm sitting on the couch and working through some of the middle chapters in my crime novel. That is, my *attempt* at a crime novel. It's a bit of a headache at the moment. There are so many glaring plot holes that it's embarrassing, and if it keeps going like this, the only crime will be my crappy writing. The middle is always hard. Same thing happens when I'm writing anything – an essay, a short story, and now a novel. Tying up the initial premise with the conclusion – it doesn't come easy. Threading it all together? That's where the magic happens, and right now I'm working in the baggy middle of a magic-free zone.

I stare at the screen. The cursor is blinking, and nothing's coming. There's no flow, and it feels like a giant wall has been erected in my mind, blocking the road between problem and solution.

I stab the keys with an angry finger.

Fuck you.

Billie Jean leaps onto the armrest, then snuggles up beside me on the couch. Brogan's snoring on the armchair on the other side of the room. It's a good day to be inside. There's a bleak, grey blanket of Scottish sky visible from the window. A heavy wind is blowing. This is doomsday weather.

Billie flops onto her side, pawing at my arm for attention like she used to do all the time when she was a kitten. Then she's momentarily distracted by a bird flying past the window. I, on the other hand, am distracted all the time.

I tap my fingers on the keyboard, desperate to type something.

Fuck you. Fuck this. Fuck you. FUCK THIS!!

I hit delete and stare at the blank page again. The floorboards creak in the hallway. *It's the wind,* I tell myself. The wind is always making weird noises in this old house. Sometimes it sounds like the roof is slowly peeling itself off the rest of the structure. The walls. The floor. Everything is so loud. This is the noisiest house I've ever lived in by far.

I stare at the blank screen. Bonus – now I'm getting a headache too. Where are my blue-light glasses when I need them? Where's my inspiration when I need that?

"What the hell am I doing?" I whisper. "I gave up my job for *this*?"

I sigh and lean my back against the armrest. About the fifteenth time I've shifted position in as many minutes.

"Oh Dan, you landed on your feet when you hooked up with me, didn't you? What a catch I am."

Billie meows.

"It's nowhere near dinnertime," I tell her. "Just lie there and be cute."

She meows again.

"What is it, Billie?"

The house groans. Billie's not looking at me anymore. She's up in a sitting position now, her attention on the living-room door, which is closed, blocking my view of the hallway. I watch her for a moment. Her ears are pricked up. She doesn't normally give the creaky floorboards this much attention.

I look at the door.

The floorboards in the hallway creak again. I'm well aware there was no gust of wind outside to trigger it.

Billie and I watch the door for a full minute.

Another one. Sounds like a giant belch from inside the walls. And I know exactly where that particular sound is coming from, too. That's the high-pitched groan that's unique to the boards in the middle of the hallway, in between our bedroom and the living-room door. I hear it every single day but usually when …

Usually when someone is walking over it.

The living room fills with cold air. I look at the door and don't dare to blink. Then I glance over at Brogan, just to make sure that he didn't get up and start plodding around the hallway. But he's still asleep on the armchair. He's not making any noise, and he's definitely not on the wander right now.

It's just the house, I tell myself. *The house is loud. It has a personality.*

"Dan? Is that you?"

I don't even remember closing the door. Did I do that? Do I usually do that when I'm working in the living room?

"Dan?"

Did he come back? He did mention something about a scratchy throat this morning when he woke up. Maybe he's getting a second dose of that bug that got in the way of our Glencoe trip. He could've walked in without me hearing him, right? Even though I'm not working with headphones on today.

Maybe. Maybe. Maybe.

Or maybe there's someone else in the house.

I hear it again. Not the big belching board but one of the quiet ones. That's the one right behind the living-room door. Brogan must've heard it too because he's finally lifted his head off the cushion, and now he's looking at the door as if expecting someone to come in. He looks at me as if to say, *Is someone else in the house, Mum?*

It's not Dan. Dan would have answered when I called him. He also would've sent me a text to let me know he was coming back from work early. He texts me whenever he leaves at his normal time. *Leaving now.* There's no way he'd skip communicating with me under special circumstances.

Billie Jean is still staring at the door.

"It's the house," I whisper to her. "It's temperamental."

This doesn't feel right. Doesn't feel safe. I lift the laptop off my legs and lower it onto the table. Slowly. Quietly. *There's nothing there*, I tell myself as I swing my legs over the edge of the couch. Not for one second do my eyes leave the door. Specifically, the door handle. I'm just waiting for it to move.

I stand up, and the house is silent now. A lone bead of sweat is slowly trickling down the side of my face. My heart is banging like a drum. I give Billie Jean a head rub, and it's not for her sake – it's for mine.

The thought of the living-room door swinging open makes me feel sick. What then? Will I be confronted by a masked intruder standing in my house?

What if it's a serial killer?
What if it's a rapist?
What if it's an insane dognapper?
"GET OUT!"
I sprint to the door like I'm out the blocks at the Olympics. Billie freaks out at this sudden movement and leaps over the back of the couch and disappears towards the kitchen. Brogan stays put, but he watches me like I'm crazy. I run to the door, grab the handle, turn it and yank the door open. I'm prepared for just about anything.
I'm staring into an empty hallway.
"Hello?"
There's no one there. I look down the length of the hallway towards the bedrooms, and it's nothing but empty space. Two rugs on the floor, covered in dog and cat hair. Framed pictures on the wall.
"Is anyone there?"
I'm coiled like a spring and ready to pounce as I walk through the house. Heart still going crazy. Dripping sweat and shaking like a leaf. I go into every room, open wardrobe doors and get down on my knees to look under the bed. When that's done, I go into the kitchen; then I check the back garden.
Someone *was* in the house. Someone might *still* be in the house.
I walk to the end of the garden path and stand at the gate, looking down both sides of the road. There's nothing unusual out here, just a row of parked cars. There's a dogwalker with a Labrador on the other side of the street. It's picture-postcard suburbia.
There's an echo of cruel laughter in the next gust of wind. Is something taunting me? It feels like it.

I hurry back up the path and close the door behind me. My back remains pressed against the door, yet I still don't feel safe. One more check around the house. Then I go back to the front door and lock it. Double-check it's locked. After that, I jam the key into the lock and leave it there.

Then I call the police.

WELL, that was a mistake.

I was still in a panic when I made the phone call, and I worded it all wrong. I told the operator that someone was in the house – as in the intruder was *still* in the house. That's what it felt like when I was making the call even though I'd checked the house multiple times over.

I was standing at the door waiting when they came with sirens blaring. A man and woman in police uniform charged up the path and hammered at the door like they were the drugs squad on a bust. They came in. Looked around. I think they expected a lot more, and when I explained the situation, rather than sympathising with me, they were clearly pissed off. Both of them.

"Didn't you tell the operator that someone was in the house?" the male officer asks. He's looking at me like I've scratched my key along the side of his car. His tone is gruff, the deep "on-duty" voice booming with irritation.

"I got mixed up on the phone," I say, standing in the hallway, fists clenched at my sides. "I thought someone *was* in the house."

"And what made you think that?" the female officer asks.

Seriously? We've already gone over this at least three

times. How many different ways do I have to say the same thing?

"I was working in the living room," I say. "I heard the floorboards creak, and it sounded very much like someone was walking around in the hallway."

The male officer glares at me. "But you didn't see anyone?"

"No."

"So it could've just been the floorboards? Old houses like these tend to make a bit of a racket in the wind."

The churning sensation in the pit of my stomach is in full swing. I can see where this is going, and without a single piece of evidence to suggest that someone was in the house, I can't stop it. This conversation feels like damage control.

"I don't think so," I say. "I know the difference between the wind and someone walking around the house."

The female officer steps closer. I think she's about to pat me on the shoulder like I'm a child in need of reassurance. "Just a wee mistake, wasn't it?"

"That's one way of putting it." The man is stone-faced. "Wasting police time – that's another."

My mouth is hanging open. Literally, like I'm waiting to catch flies. Am I in the wrong for calling the police when I was frightened? When I was convinced that there was an intruder in my house?

The male officer's intense stare isn't helping. What is this guy's problem? I see the other officer backing off towards the door like she's seen enough. Her partner, PC Pissed Off, doesn't move.

He grunts at me. "Next time be a little more careful, okay?"

There's no sympathy in his eyes.

"Let's go, Ryan," the woman says. "No harm done this time."

Oh shit. The way he's looking at me. He knows he's got me and that he's right about no one else being in the house, but does he have to look at me like *that*? I might have overreacted, but I thought I was doing the right thing. Being safe.

Why are the police making *me* feel like a criminal?

"Sorry," I mumble. Right now, I just want him out of my house.

"Are you okay?" the woman asks. She stops at the door, turning back to me. Now she's the one giving me the hard stare. It's not a well-intentioned question about my well-being either. She's asking me, without asking me, if I'm on something.

"What?"

"I said, are you okay?"

My face feels like it's on fire. I'm convinced they're going to put me in handcuffs and arrest me for wasting police time. I clearly haven't done a very good job of convincing them of how scared I am. Maybe if they knew about George Square, it would be different. But I'm not going there. There's a part of me that wants to believe I overreacted. That would be much easier to stomach than the thought of an intruder in broad daylight.

"I'm fine," I say.

Of course, that's the biggest lie of all.

CHAPTER NINE

It's back to being a delivery driver that night. Back in the car, which sometimes feels like the safest place of all.

I didn't get much writing done during the day. Not after freaking out like I did back in the house. Even now, I'm still not entirely convinced either way. The rational part of me wants to believe it was the wind making the floorboards creak and that our old house is just a noisy bugger. Still, the police saw right through me. They saw my uncertainty and made me feel like shit for it.

So yeah, I'll take the car. I'll take the open road and the mind-numbing job of delivering food to strangers.

Except, tonight is going too well.

I'm three hours into what's supposed to be a long night shift. It's a little after nine o'clock, and I'm parked in a quiet residential street in the well-to-do suburb of Lenzie, close to where I delivered my last order.

Half an hour ago, before dropping off that order, I received a text from a rep working for the company I deliver for. Someone has made a complaint against me. A *formal* complaint. The customer is accusing me of "aggressive behaviour" and claims that I intimidated them on their doorstep after a disagreement about where I dropped off the bag with their food in it. According to this anonymous complainer, we had a verbal argument, which ended with me throwing "scalding hot" chips in their face and calling them all sorts of names.

There's one problem. None of it happened. But I have to address it, and that means calling the rep back.

Now I'm sitting in the driver's seat with the phone pressed tight against my ear. I can't quite believe what the man on the other end of the call is saying to me. He speaks with a soft Indian accent, and he talks to me like he's reading from a script. He's calm and polite, but it feels like I'm talking to a machine.

"So, do you understand the accusation made against you?" he says.

"Not really."

"Are you denying that it happened?"

I'm doing my best not to lose my temper. Lots of deep breaths and thinking back to any little snippets of information about mindfulness that I've picked up over the years. I leave a pause before answering. "Are you kidding me? This never happened. Someone is telling blatant lies."

"And yet this is the information we received."

"The information you received is wrong. How many ways do I have to say it? This did not happen."

"So you *are* denying it?"

Deep breath, Angie.

"That's right," I tell him. "I'm denying it. Did this person send you any evidence? Photos?"

"There was photographic evidence."

I frown. "Of what?"

"We have several photos of chips scattered outside the customer's house."

I almost laugh out loud. "Chips? You've got photos of chips?"

"Yes."

"That's all?"

"Yes."

I'm this close to pinching myself on the back of the hand. Really fucking hard. It'll hurt, but at least it'll tell me if I'm dreaming or not. Seriously? Do they believe this accusation because someone sent them photos of chips in a garden? Yet the scary thing is it sounds like they do believe it. Otherwise, what's the point of this phone call? I threw chips at a faceless customer because they claimed I left their bag of food in the wrong place. Guilty until proven innocent.

"Are you still there, miss?"

"Oh yes," I say. "I'm still here."

The rep starts to talk, but I cut him off. The irritation in my voice is obvious.

"Okay," I say. "So let me see if I understand this complaint. I went to someone's house this evening, left the bag in the wrong place, and we got into an argument about it. Is that correct?"

"Correct."

"You've tracked my orders. I was definitely at this person's house?"

"That's right."

Chips ... chips ... chips. Where did I deliver chips to? It's been a busy night, and I've made so many stops so far that I can't recall everything off the top of my head. There's been a few regulars, and apart from them, everyone else was new.

A name jumps into my head.

Martha Hunt.

Is she involved here?

Was I at her door tonight? Could've been, I guess. Or did she order from someone else's house to cover her tracks? I wonder if the agency fired her, and now she's trying to get me fired as payback. Where does she live? Did she tell us where she lived? I wish I'd paid more attention to my stops tonight, but I wasn't exactly expecting a complaint. So far this evening, there's only been one face-to-face drop-off, and that was a sixty-something guy who'd ordered pizza. He was delightful and gave me a generous cash tip. Everything else was leave-at-the-door. I haven't seen any other customers tonight.

Would she do that? A cold feeling of dread forms in the pit of my stomach. I think about the push in George Square. I think about the intruder. The missing photo album.

No. I push the thought away. Martha may be a crappy house sitter, but she's not *that* level of psycho. Still, she might be responsible for "Chipgate". An eye for an eye. She loses her job, so I have to lose mine.

I can't think. It would be so much easier to get a firmer grasp of this if the robot on the other end of the line opened up a little.

"Can you tell me anything else about the order?" I ask. "Anything besides … *chips*."

"I'm afraid not."

"How am I supposed to defend myself if you won't give me the name and address of the person who made the complaint?"

"We can't provide that information."

"What about the order number?"

There's a short pause, like he's checking the script. "We can't give that out either. You'd be able to find out the name and address easily from there, and we must protect customer privacy."

What about protecting your drivers from bullshit accusations? What about the workers? What about the people who do all the fucking legwork around here?

"You won't give me anything?"

"No."

"Well, okay then. I don't know what we're talking about." His voice is infuriatingly calm.

"You don't know what we're talking about?"

"I don't know because it didn't happen," I say, growing dizzy because of the number of circles we're talking round in here. "I'm trying to tell you that someone is falsely accusing me. Why are you so quick to believe my accuser and to disbelieve me?"

"We have to take all complaints seriously."

"In case you get a bad review?"

"We pride ourselves on top-quality customer experience, miss."

Circles. Endless fucking circles. I get it. He's not listening to a word I'm saying, and it seems like he has no intention of ever doing so. All he's doing is repeating words from the generic script he's been given to deal with situations like this. Words that have no meaning. Words that aren't going anywhere. I don't want to get mad at him because he's most likely just an average joe working long hours for shitty pay.

Chips. Fucking chips!

A man in a long winter coat walks past the car along with a chocolate-coloured labradoodle on an extendable leash. The man and I exchange awkward looks. Then he's gone. The man smokes the last of his cigarette while the dog sniffs the outskirts of one of the well-manicured nature strips that furnish the pavement.

"Okay," I say to the rep, wishing that I had a cigarette too, even though I quit more than twenty years ago. "Please listen to me."

"I *am* listening to you."

"I think I know who's responsible for this. There's a woman with a grudge against me, and I think she's the one lashing out. It's a long story, but we had a little ... *disagreement* ... about a housesitting job she was scheduled to do for me. Things got ugly. I made a formal complaint, and now, as well as other things, she's fabricating a story to get back at me. It *was* a woman who complained tonight, wasn't it?"

"I can't give you that information."

Fucker. Put the script away.

"Her name is Martha Hunt," I say. "You don't have to confirm, but does that name, umm, ring any bells?"

"I'm afraid—"

I almost punch the dashboard. What's frustrating is that I don't know anything for sure. I haven't seen Martha since she walked out of our house in disgrace. What if it's not her? All this guy needs to do is give me a name and I'll know for sure.

"I know. You can't confirm."

"Correct."

"Don't I have the right to know who's making accusations against me?" I ask.

"We can't give out names. I'm very sorry."

This conversation is so ridiculous that I'm almost laughing. But if any laughter comes, it won't be a happy sound. "Do you even care what's true here?"

"Yes, of course."

I roll down the window to let in some fresh air. It's cold, but it's a welcome slap in the face from nature. I can still smell the leftovers from the labradoodle man's cigarette. Feel the old cravings.

"Please listen to me," I say. "I've made thousands of deliveries for you guys, and I've never had a single complaint. Not before tonight. Do you know why? Because I'm good at my job. It's not brain surgery, is it? I know how to collect an order from a restaurant and drop it off at someone's house. Once there, I either knock and hand it over or leave it at their door as requested. I'm polite. I'm respectful. And please believe me when I tell you that I've never thrown chips at anyone in my life. Even if I was angry at a customer, it wouldn't occur to me. Can't you see that this is a prank?"

There's a long pause.

"We'd just like you to remember our code of conduct when you deliver for us. That's all we're concerned with right now."

"Do you believe me?" I ask in a pleading tone. "Do you believe me when I say I didn't do this? That someone is lying. That someone has made all of this up."

"We don't know—"

"No, not *we*. Do *you* believe me?"

That makes him hesitate.

"I'm sorry. It's not my ... I wasn't there."

My words are hitting a brick wall. The rep isn't interested in whether or not someone has a grudge against me. He's just here to give me a telling-off because that's the protocol. I guess I should be grateful they're not firing me. At least, I hope they're not. They do have photos of chips, after all.

"Okay," I say, leaning back in the driver's seat. I roll up the window, as it's freezing inside the car now. "What happens next?"

"Nothing. Your behaviour has been excellent so far, and this is just a—"

"A warning?"

"A clarification."

It's so ludicrous I almost laugh out loud.

"Okay."

The most pointless phone call of my life ends, and I sit in the car, staring out at an endless ocean of quiet suburbia. This neighbourhood is tidy, but there's something soulless about it. This is the sort of place I would've ended up in if I'd stuck it out with the marketing job. Still, they'll be warm and cosy in their nice houses. They don't need to work a shitty delivery job because of some stupid dream about becoming a writer.

"Was that you, Martha?" I whisper.

I should've asked the robot if any single customer made a lot of separate orders and subsequent cancellations tonight. Was that how she found me? She must've figured out the area I delivered, then ordered stuff until I came up as her delivery driver. Before that, she probably made a bunch of orders and cancelled when she saw someone else was delivering. But she did get me in the end. I dropped off the order, and then Martha threw chips all over the garden, took photos and made her crazy complaint. I can see her doing it. Hoping it would get me fired.

How did she even know that I deliver food at night? I

don't remember us talking about work or anything like that. It never came up.

I shudder even though the car is heating up again. What if she's following me around? If she was following me, she could've seen me at work. Waited for me to drive away after dropping off an order, then hurried up to someone's doorstep and took note of the company name that's printed on the delivery bags.

Nah, that's ridiculous. Maybe it's just bad luck, all this weird stuff that's happening.

I bury my head in my hands and let rip with a silent scream. Then I look at the rows of nice houses again. Nice gardens, nice cars. Tonight, that feeling of regret about my life choices is stronger than ever. Right now, I'm failing.

I scold myself yet again for turning my back on a well-paying job to live this sort of hand-to-mouth life.

When will I learn? Risks are for other people.

CHAPTER TEN

I get home about three o'clock in the morning after what felt like an interminable shift. At least the rest of the night was uneventful, thank God.

I'm exhausted, but all I manage is four hours of broken sleep. There's an underlying anxiety gnawing away at me, and it's especially noticeable when I'm lying awake in bed, staring up at the ceiling. Nothing but my thoughts to keep me company. It feels like butterflies in my stomach. Butterflies with teeth.

At seven o'clock, I lie in bed, listening to Dan rattling around in the kitchen, making himself breakfast. Feeling too warm under the sheets, I get up, telling myself that I've got a good day of writing ahead of me.

I plod towards the kitchen, my feet loud and heavy. The floor creaks underneath me. I've already made the decision not to tell Dan about the complaint. I know it's wrong to keep him in the dark like this, but I don't want him to worry, and despite all this recent weirdness in my life, I still believe things will get better.

It's November fifteenth, I tell myself. *It's a curse.*

The kitchen is bright, and I squint my eyes in protest at the sunlight seeping in through the window. It feels like sharp needles poking at my eyeballs. Dan's sitting at the table, sipping coffee and eating toast. He's scrolling on his phone, and as I walk in, he looks up, his eyebrows arching in surprise.

"Look out," he says, grinning. "It's night of the living dead."

I give him the finger.

Dan laughs. "And a very good morning to you too. Didn't think I'd be seeing you before I left the house."

My voice is hoarse. "Me neither."

He takes a fresh bite of toast, and it sounds like fireworks exploding in my head. "You got back late last night."

I pull a chair and sit down. A ferocious yawn escapes out of me. "Did I?"

"You did."

"About three, I think."

"It was closer to four."

"If you say so."

Dan glances at his watch. "How was work?"

"Umm, fine."

He nods. "Can I get you anything before I go?"

I look at the kettle and toaster on the counter. They might as well be on the other side of the world. "No, I'll grab something later. You finish your breakfast."

I want to talk to him. I want to talk to him, yet I don't. But we've always been open with one another, and I know I should tell him about George Square, the police and the non-intruder and now the complaint at work. But I can't. It feels less real if I keep it to myself, and I remind myself, a little forcefully, that it's probably done and dusted now. No need to worry Dan. He'll blame it on the time of year, and he'd probably be right.

Things do get a little weird at this time of year, don't they? Right, Dan. I swear to God I'm cursed.

Still, I was on edge last night after the complaint and that frustrating (to put it mildly) conversation with the rep. On top of that, I had that weird sensation of being followed. Of being watched. Checking over my shoulder every five minutes to see if there was a pair of headlights behind me on the road. Every time I left the car to drop off an order, I made sure to take extra photos of the bag on the doorstep. Intact. No chips were harmed in this delivery or that one or the one after it. I even filmed a couple of drop-offs for extra security. And I was quick about everything.

It'll be fine.

No need to tell Dan.

I stand up, open the fridge and stare inside. I take out a carton of orange juice and pour myself a glass. Then I sit down at the table, and although I should be hungry after not eating much last night, the thought of food is impossible.

Dan smiles across the table. It's one of those *I've got something to tell you* smiles. "Oh, I nearly forgot. Something very strange happened last night."

I can feel the butterflies. Their sharp teeth biting harder into my nervous system. Still, I try to sound calm and even curious.

"What happened?"

"Well," Dan says, "let's just say we got a surprise package on the doorstep."

I look down into the glass of orange juice. At the floating

juicy bits that I can't stand. Why do we keep buying this pulpy crap?

My grip tightens on the freezing glass.

"A package."

Dan does a finger drumroll on the table. He brings it to a sudden stop when he sees I'm not amused.

"Your photo album."

I gawp at him, unable to speak.

"It's back," he says. "We've got it back."

"My album? It just showed up?"

Dan nods. "Sure did. Imagine my surprise when I opened the door and saw it lying on the doorstep."

"It was just lying on the doorstep?"

"Yep."

"What time did this happen?"

"About eight o'clock. I was dozing on the couch, half watching a David Attenborough thing on Netflix. You know how his voice always soothes me to sleep. It was about gorillas in—"

"Dan!"

"Okay, okay. I heard something outside, but there was no one there when I opened the door. Just the album."

"It *has* to be her," I mumble to myself.

"What's that?" Dan asks.

"Martha. She took it."

"I suppose she could've taken it by mistake," Dan says.

I wipe a smudge off the side of my glass like it's an important thing to do. Anything to hide the discomfort that feels like it's showing on my face.

"By mistake?"

"She must have packed it by mistake when she was

taking her things out of the drawer. Considering what happened, it was nice of her to bring it back."

I clench a fist under the table.

"*Nice?*"

"Well, she didn't have to do it. Right? I'd have left it on the doorstep if I were her. I know she messed up and all, but we did catch her in a, well, a rather embarrassing situation."

My mind is a swirling bubble of noise. It's too early in the day to deal with this.

Was it nice of her? Maybe Martha had nothing to do with all that other stuff, and maybe I do owe her one for bringing the album back. It was a mistake. Whether it was deliberate or not, I can't help but feel ... *violated*. That's the only word that springs to mind. That album, the photos and my writings, it's not for anyone else to see.

"Where is it?" I ask.

Dan points to the kitchen counter behind me. "Ta-da!"

I glance over my shoulder, and the photo album is there on top of the microwave. It's home. I look at Dan, then back at the album. I repeat this three times to the point where it must look like I'm trying to unscrew my head from my shoulders.

"What the hell?"

I push back the chair and stand up so fast it's like royalty just entered the room. The chair legs scrape off the floor and make a howling noise. I grab my album off the microwave, and a frantic skim through the pages reveals that nothing is missing, at least nothing that I can see at first glance. I skim again and don't blink. Everything seems to be there. All the photos in their sleeves and also the folded sheets of paper at the back with my writings.

There's a flood of relief. But it's short-lived.

I have to know for sure.

"You definitely didn't see anyone at the door?" I ask. "In the garden? On the street?"

"No."

"And there wasn't a note with the album?"

"Nothing."

Shit.

"Martha must have lifted it by mistake," Dan says again. He goes on to repeat himself because, deep down, he wants it to make sense too. If only he knew the half of it. "She must have been using the top drawer for her clothes and ended up putting the album into her bag along with her things. A note would've been good, I agree. But we did leave things a little ... awkward."

Dan's smile is hard to decipher. Hard to know if he believes that fairy tale or not.

A mistake? Really?

I sit down at the kitchen table with the album in front of me. I look at it like it's a vial with a deadly virus inside.

Did you spill my secrets?

The album was buried under a pile of my underwear in the top drawer. It's not easily taken by accident, not least because it's not the lightest thing in the world. It's not even visible without someone making an effort to rummage through my things. I wouldn't be surprised if Martha, five minutes after we took off on holiday, went digging through my belongings, found the album and had a good look at the photos and all the things I wrote. It's an excruciating thought. If she did, she knows far too much.

That's if she did steal the album. Maybe I'll go along with Dan and pretend it was an accident. Pretend that all this November madness will just blow over.

Dan gives me a sideways look over the table. "Everything okay?"

"Great," I say, taking a sip of orange juice.

Dan slurps the last of his coffee. Then he stands up, gathering his plate and cup. "I thought you'd be more excited to have it back."

"What's that?"

"I thought you'd be relieved to get the album back."

"I'm *definitely* relieved."

"Good," Dan says, stacking his plate and cup into the dishwasher. He stretches his arms above his head and yawns. I hear his joints crack. "Right. I'd better be off."

"Have a good day."

He leans back against the counter and looks at me. "You sound flat, Ang. Are you okay?"

"Just tired."

"Go back to bed, then, will you? I'm sleepy just looking at you."

I fake a big yawn.

Dan laughs. "Gotta be fresh if you're going to write that masterpiece of yours."

"Agreed."

I wave him out of the kitchen. "Have a good day. I'll spare you my morning breath and blow you a kiss instead."

He catches the kiss and smells it. Gags, then wanders off to get his work bag.

I lose the smile as soon as he leaves for work. I get up, pour the pulpy orange juice down the sink and take my photo album upstairs. After that, I'm sitting on the bed for an hour, looking through the album in fine detail. Over and over again. If I had a magnifying glass, I'd be using it. The photos are all there, all in the right order. Same with the things I wrote. Everything is where it should be, but I'm convinced that there has to be something I'm missing. There has to be s*omething* – some kind of subtle vandalism that isn't obvious at first glance. Like a message.

I lose count of how many times I go through the album. There's nothing. In the end, I snap it shut and sit there in defeat.

Of course, I tell myself. Why would she need to vandalise anything? That would prove to anyone looking in from the outside that she stole the album. That there was malice involved. Besides, she got what she wanted – information. Information about me.

She's smarter than I gave her credit for.

But really? Is Martha responsible for all this weird shit lately? I keep going back and forth, but there's no clear-cut answer. Either it's a run of bad luck. Or something more sinister is going on.

Sometimes I wonder if I made a mistake being so hard on her when we came back that day. She was naked and humiliated. I guess I could've been a little more delicate, and, likewise, it wouldn't have killed me to skip the formal complaint. Then again, she was in the wrong. Blatantly in the wrong. Consequences exist, and Martha, if she got fired, should realise that's because she should have done her job properly.

I open the top drawer and put the album back where it belongs. I blink hard. Focus, then take a step back. It feels like the wind has been knocked out of me.

My underwear has been moved.

It's subtle – it's very subtle, but I see it. This is my top drawer, and the underwear and also the socks aren't where they're supposed to be. No, this isn't quite right. Socks are folded together, always bundled to the left while the underwear is squeezed to the right. They never get mixed up, and there's always a little gap in the middle to separate them. Socks and underwear don't touch. It's a stupid quirk of mine, but it's something I've done since I was a child. I don't even have to think about it anymore. It's always the same. Always the way I've done it.

Yet the socks have been pushed towards the underwear section. And vice versa.

Something very strange is happening.

I hear Dan's voice in my head. *It's that time of year, Ang. Isn't it?*

Or is it?

Is Martha Hunt watching the house? Is she waiting for Dan and me to go out before letting herself in to perform these little gaslighting manoeuvres? She *could* do it. She could get away with it. The pets know her. Brogan wouldn't start barking if he saw her walking into the house without me or Dan around. If she got a key cut while we were away, she could do it. Just like she could push me in George Square. Just like she could let herself into the house and scare the shit out of me creaking the floorboards. Just like she could make complaints against me at my work to get me fired.

No, that's crazy talk.

I relocate the photo album, putting it into an empty shoe box and sliding the box to the back of the wardrobe. Now the box is buried under a pile of old clothes that are long overdue a trip to the charity shop.

I rush to the front door and turn the handle. Dan locked it. I double-, triple-check anyway. Same with the back door. Then it's back to the hallway, and I stand there, looking back and forth between the living room and the bedroom. I imagine her walking around when no one is in. The thrill it must give her. The sense of power.

And how does it feel walking around when there *is* someone here? Like me. Like she might've done yesterday.

Oh, Angie, you must be going crazy. One too many November fifteenths, sweetie. It's in the family, after all.

I return to the bedroom, approaching the top drawer like I'm wading into shark-infested waters. I'm freaking myself out. Too much time alone in the house, that's all. Why would Martha sneak in and move my socks from one side of the drawer to another? It's such a subtle gesture – too subtle. It could just be Dan taking clothes out of the dryer and throwing them into the wrong place. I might've even done it myself. I have been distracted.

This is my head. Back and forth. Martha, November fifteenth, Martha, November fifteenth.

One thing I'm sure of. The house doesn't feel safe.

I check the locks again. Check the garden. The street.

Back in the house, I grab the front door key from the hook and slot it into the keyhole. Then I go into the laundry room and find a box of jumbo-sized washing powder. I push it into the hallway, my legs bent at the knees. I slide the box over towards the front door, position it in the centre and step back, studying my work. A roadblock. It'll do for now. There's no way that Martha (or any intruder) can get in. If she tries to insert a key, she'll have to knock the other one out of the keyhole first, and that's hard to do with this particular lock. Even if she gets the key out, she'll have a hell of a job pushing the door open with that jumbo box of washing powder sitting in front of it.

I'll jam a chair under the doorknob in the kitchen too. Keep the back door safe.

Just to be sure.

I take several walks between the hallway and the kitchen, checking the doors. Just to be sure, just to be sure.

It's probably nothing.

It's still early, but I'm not sure how much writing I'm going to get done. That'll be two days in a row where I've done nothing.

"Books don't write themselves, Angie."

I stand at the front door, scrutinising the details of my improvised barricades. I imagine someone trying to force their way in. I guess if they were determined enough, it could happen.

I take a step back. Stare at the door handle and imagine her chubby little fingers pulling it down from the outside.

Who's a good boy? You're a good boy, aren't you? You love your auntie Martha, don't you, boy? Yes, you do.

What would Dan say if I suggested changing the locks?

LATER THAT MORNING, I sit down at the desk with a large cup of coffee. Try to get some writing done. It's painful. I can't concentrate, and the more I try to force it, the more painful it becomes. I hate everything about the work. Hate the story. I hate the way I'm writing it. To hell with sitting here, rocking back and forth on my chair, staring at a screen and feeling like the worst writer who ever lived.

Screw it. I'll go out and deliver. Start early and work late into the night again. Maybe I'll throw chips in someone's face.

Before that, I take Brogan for a throw-the-ball session in the park. He's exhausted, and after feeding him and Billie

Jean, I fill my rucksack with snacks and bottled water and take it out to the car. Maybe I'll grab a coffee on the road.

I leave the TV on in the living room. Turn it up so that if anyone comes to the front door, they'll think someone's at home. The chair is still wedged on the doorknob at the back door, and I'm not sure how Dan will take that when he comes in. But I have to take the washing powder away and remove the key from the lock to get out the front door. It'll be okay. Dan will be home in a few hours.

Delivering is easy. It's everything else that feels hard right now. The orders come in, and I only work the jobs I want to work. Still, if I don't accept orders, then I don't get paid. I drive around town, ticking off orders. I work fast. Ping-ping-PING! There's always someone wanting to eat without leaving the house. Might as well be me who brings them lunch. Brings them dinner.

After three hours straight, I drive to one of my quiet residential streets in the suburbs. One of my "chill spots". There are massive overhanging trees, all stripped of their summer leaves and waiting for springtime to bring them back to life. The street is silent except for infrequent spurts of birdsong and the occasional passing car.

I sip on a large takeaway coffee, but the caffeine isn't working fast enough. My eyes grow heavy. This is what happens when I don't get enough sleep.

I'm tired. So tired.

And unfortunately for me, my mind wanders. It wanders back to that day when I was seven years old. Back to that day when my life changed forever.

CHAPTER ELEVEN

Something's wrong with Mummy.

I don't understand why she's pretending not to hear me. I'm banging on the window at the front of the house. It hurts, and my hands are swelling up like balloons, but I won't stop hitting the glass.

"Mummy! It's me. It's Angie!"

What's she doing? I can see through the gap in the curtains, and it doesn't make sense. She's walking around the living room and won't let me in. Even from here, I see the black emptiness in her eyes. I've seen it before.

"I've come home early, Mummy. The headteacher couldn't get you on the phone. I'm not feeling well. Why didn't you answer? Why didn't you pick up?"

Something's wrong with Mummy. She doesn't notice the empty cupboards or when we run out of toilet paper or wonder why we have no salt or why the grass is so long and wild at the back of the house. It's like a jungle. Now it's my job to notice these things. That's become the new normal. I have to run down to the shop and get bread and jam when there's nothing else to eat. Biscuits, sweets and crackers. I have to find out who can fix broken toilets. Dad was horrible at DIY, yet she misses him so much.

I try the handle again, but I can't get in. Front and back doors are locked. I don't have a key, and Mum always lets me in when I come back from school. It's only a short walk from the house to the school. Sometimes she comes to meet me at the school gate. Those are the good days, but I know when she's not there that her eyes are black. She always lets me in, and today she can't even hear me. It's like she's put on a mask, and it scares me. But I'm not going anywhere. I'm hitting the door. I'm hitting the windows at the living room, where I can still see her through the gap. This isn't supposed to happen. We live in a nice street with detached houses. Her own parents used to live here and left her the house when they died. Nice street, nice houses and nice neighbours.

We're supposed to be happy.

"Mummy!"

Something is wrong. Something is always wrong. I can't get into the house, and I don't know what to do. There's no one else to talk to or ask for help. I've got an auntie on Dad's side, but she stopped coming round to visit a long time ago. Aunt Rose on Mum's side lives so far away. Ever since Mum stopped working, she hasn't had friends. I don't know how we've got the money to last this long. Don't know if she had savings or if my other grandparents were sending it to her to keep us going. We don't belong in a nice street like this.

She's indoors all the time. Bad moods and silence. Her skin is turning grey, and she looks older than her real age. She needs fresh air and friends. What she doesn't need is staying in bed for days and staring at the ceiling. I play her favourite music, The Beatles, and hope it'll wake her up again. It doesn't. I know it's bad when playing The Beatles doesn't work. The dishes are piling up in the sink. The smell is bad – so bad. I hate the sight of a messy house (and the smell!), but it's so hard to keep up with all this cleaning and shopping while still going to school and doing my homework. I can't tell the teachers. I don't know what I'm supposed to say to them.

She always comes back. But it's been too long this time.

"Mummy, please. I've got a fresh loaf in my bag. I'll make sandwiches. I'll make tea."

I don't have any bread in my bag. I'm not well, and I came straight home from school after convincing the headteacher, Mrs Thorpe, that I was okay to walk by myself.

No bread, but it might get her to open the door.

Where are all the neighbours? Where's Mr Watson from number ten? He's nice, and I need someone bigger than me to kick down the door. Like they do in films.

What if I scream?

Why didn't I tell someone that things were getting worse? It's not just Dad. She hated her job, working in a bakery. Life didn't pan out the way she'd planned it. I think she gave up on her dream of being a singer when she became pregnant with me. She never said it was my fault, but someone, I can't remember who, said a light went out in her eyes over the years. I wasn't in the plan. Mum never made me feel bad about it, and she always said she loved me, but I didn't make her happy. Not like dreams can. Everything got heavier, and she stopped being Mummy. She just couldn't summon the energy. The light. The love. Black clouds ate up the blue skies, and now she's lying in bed all day. I'm only seven, but I feel so tired. I'm always on – I have to be switched on. There's no one else to help.

Finally, she looks at me.

"Go away, Angie. You don't want to see this."

I'm stunned. It's like someone in a film turning and speaking directly to you through the screen. Her voice is muffled. Low-pitched, almost unrecognisable. I realise for the first time that she's done her hair nice and that she's wearing makeup. She's even got a nice dress on. It scares me. Something's so very wrong, and I don't know what to do. Fear and confusion make me bang the window harder, and I can't feel the pain in my balloon hands anymore.

"Mummy, let me in."

"Go back to school."

"LET ME IN."

Something is wrong with Mummy.

What should I do? There's a horrible feeling in my stomach like I'm going to throw up. Do I go next door? We don't talk to the neighbours much, even though they're nice people, so will they even know who I am?

I wish I had a brother or a sister. Or maybe not. I'd have to share this with them, and this isn't nice.

My palms are flat against the glass. My arms heavy after all the pounding.

"Mummy! *Pleeeeease.*"

She looks like an old woman gliding across the floor, but she isn't old. She's thirty-something, I think. Thirty-what? It's old but not ancient. What's that in her hand? What's she holding? Some kind of can ... some kind of container.

"Go away, Angie."

That empty, hollow voice. It sounds like a man's voice. Where is her voice?

She comes over and puts a hand on the glass. I do the same. Now we're touching hands, sort of. She pulls the curtains over but doesn't do it properly. She's left a gap at the bottom.

"Don't look," she calls back. "This isn't your fault."

I kneel to get a better view. My nose is squashed against the glass, but I press harder until it hurts, and even then I don't stop. I try to hit the glass, but my arms are two sticks of cement. I look into the gloomy living room. What's she doing? It's so dark in there. Why is she pouring that stuff out of the can all over her nice dress? Something's wrong. There's nothing in her eyes. They're like a doll's eyes. She doesn't react to being wet like a normal person would.

"Mummy!"

I hit the glass harder. I'm too scared to run to the neighbours. I can't take my eyes off her, and I keep hitting the glass and hoping that somehow I can break it.

"HELP!"

That noise. I know what that noise is. Mummy's struck a match.

"Don't look."

WHOOOSH!

The deep roar I hear – that I *feel* – is like nothing I've ever heard or felt before. It's like some giant monster waking up underneath the ground. My first thought is that there's an earthquake. I learned about earthquakes at schools and a thing called the Richter scale that measures the strength of earthquakes. This is not an earthquake. This is fire. This is the house on fire.

This is Mummy on fire.

She's screaming, and I know she regrets what she's done. She regrets striking the match. Regrets choosing to leave me.

I know already that the house will burn for hours.

Mummy will never sing again.

I'm screaming too.

The heat is coming through. I feel it on my face, and I know it's going to get worse. Bigger. Hotter. Mummy's running around the living room like a mad, fiery octopus. Arms flapping. She trips over the couch, and now that's on fire too.

I don't notice the neighbours running towards me. The first thing I hear is a man's voice in my ear. A deep, booming voice, yet he sounds as scared as I feel. His voice cracks. I think he's crying.

"GET HER OUT OF HERE!"

Strong hands grab me at the waist. I'm up in the air, spinning around. They're pulling me away from the house. I see people at the window. Mr Watson is there too, and he's got this bug-eyed look of horror on his face. Someone else throws up on the grass. They're all looking through the window, and the nice woman from next door is the first to scream. She backs off down the driveway, crossing herself like people do in church.

"Oh God," she says. "Oh God in Heaven."

I'm pulled further and further away, and I hear people coughing behind me. There's a lot of shouting. A short while later, the first of the sirens are wailing in the distance.

I smell the smoke and see it thick and black, rising from the house and towards the sky.

I wave because that's Mummy floating up to Heaven.

CHAPTER TWELVE

Billie Jean is gone.

She's been missing since this morning, and it's almost four o'clock in the afternoon. What little light there is left outside is disappearing fast.

I'm standing at the front door again. Calling her name. Desperate for a glimpse of her tabby and white coat coming towards me while at the same time pushing back a feeling of icy dread that's been sawing away at my innards for hours.

"Billie! Billie Jean!"

My voice is shrill with panic.

I can't call Dan. I don't want to worry him, but I think, more than that, when I call him, that's when it'll become real. And I'm sure she'll turn up at any second. Even though I've been saying the same thing to myself ever since late morning when she didn't show up for her second breakfast.

"BILLIE!"

It's getting so dark. I can feel the bite of winter coming in early. She can't stay out all night in this, and more importantly, she *wouldn't* stay out all night in this.

I stare out towards the street. At the boundaries of Billie's known world – a world of parked cars, well-trimmed hedges, various types of garden furniture and wooden fences. What if a dog got her? We've got plenty of them around here. There's that Alsatian across the street, and I've always been a little worried when I see Billie cross the road and strut off in that direction. She's too cocky. Too confident. When did I last see her? Dan told me before he left for work that she'd gone out early after not eating much. That must have been around nine hours ago. Nine hours! She must be starving.

"Where are you?" I whisper.

I've walked up and down the street more times than I can remember, calling her name. I don't care if the neighbours think I'm mad. But she's nowhere to be seen. Nothing. That's not like her. She never ignores me, at least not for this long. This isn't the normal cat going out for hours at a time thing. Something's happened, and I'm already planning a major search party in my mind. Printing out the "Missing Cat" posters, notifying the appropriate groups and pages online, and I've picked out a suitable (and recent) photo for the job.

It's the next thing, isn't it? After all the other recent incidents. This is the next thing that's going wrong.

What if I'm bringing all this bad luck upon myself? What if I'm blowing everything out of proportion? Am I okay? I don't feel okay.

I should never have been so on-and-off with therapy. And maybe the group thing was never enough anyway. Maybe I should start seeing someone on a one-to-one basis like I did when I was a child.

"BILLIE JEAN!"

Writing is definitely not happening today. I've watched TV, and I can't remember a single thing that was on the screen. I've wasted time on my phone, reading articles and Reddit forums about cats going missing. Some people have lost their cats for days, weeks, months and, in some extreme cases, even years. It's not comforting.

I haven't taken Brogan for a walk because I can't leave the house in case Billie Jean comes back. I won't be able to go to work tonight either.

There's no sign of her out there.

Well, I'm done. I can't deal with this alone anymore. I have to call Dan, and maybe he can get started on printing the flyers and posters while he's still in the office. And while I'm waiting for him to come home, I'll start knocking on doors up and down the street. Maybe she's locked in someone's shed or garage. Hungry. Thirsty. Calling for help. I'll turn this street upside down if I have to and even if all the neighbours hate my guts for it.

I try to take deep breaths. Push the panic back a little. I even try counting.

One. Two. Three.

I'm about to yell for her one last time when there's a rattling noise from inside the house. My heart stops. It sounds like the noise the pet door makes when either Billie or Brogan go through it, but it's probably Brogan, who's been going in and out more often than usual today because he didn't get a walk.

No, I think. Don't get your hopes up. Call Dan and tell him.

There's a sudden warmth at my legs. I look down, and Billie Jean is rubbing up against my shins, her tail up and hooked at the top. She looks up, meowing at me. Telling me she's hungry.

"Billie! Oh, thank God."

I scratch the top of her head.

"Where have you been?" I ask. "Billie – where have you been all day? Why didn't you come when I—?"

The snarl of a car engine interrupts me. That's followed by an explosion of acceleration that makes our quiet street sound like a Formula 1 track. While my back's turned, a vehicle races down the middle of the road.

I spin around. The flash of headlights is there and gone. I poke my head through the gap in the doorway, but it's too dark to make out the model of car. The engine fades. The lights disappear into the dark.

Billie Jean tries to make a sudden dash through my legs. I bend down and scoop her up before she can get clear. She wriggles in my arms, but my grasp is firm. Then I'm backing up, retreating into the hallway. I shove the front door closed with my back. Only then do I put Billie down.

I watch her take off towards the kitchen. *If she's been outside all day*, I think, *why would she be so desperate to go out again so soon?*

CHAPTER THIRTEEN

I fall asleep in the car again that night. That's despite another superhuman dose of caffeine. Despite a bombardment of sugary snacks on my system. Unable to keep my eyes open, I'm taking a break in the same residential street when it happens.

I dream about the house on fire again.

I don't usually sleep on the job, let alone dream about the past. But I feel so tired lately, right down to the bone. And yet work – that is, deliveries not writing – is when I feel most relaxed.

After waking up from the dream, I look at my reflection in the rear-view mirror. A pale, blotchy face looks back at me. My forehead is damp with sweat.

"Looking good," I say.

I fall back into the driver's seat. The dream felt even more real than last night. The flames hotter, the screams louder. Sometimes, looking back at the past is like trying to view an intricate painting from afar. The details are there, but none of it's close enough to affect me. Sometimes, like in these dreams, the past feels too close for comfort. That's when I'm standing right in front of the painting. Missing none of it.

I get out of the car and stretch my legs for a while. Practise a little diaphragmatic breathing. The more I walk, the better I feel, and when I get back to the Corolla, I drink about a litre of water in order to rehydrate.

The phone pings. It's an order, and I'll take it whatever it is. The customer wants a snack fest – crisps, chocolates and fizzy drinks. All the top-notch nutritional items. I accept their order and drive off. Stop in at the petrol station, grab the snacks and head north as the night sky darkens. Man, it's cold. I'll have to layer up more if I'm doing these all-nighters.

The traffic is fine. I reach the destination about twenty minutes later, and it's not pretty. We're in the badlands now. The address is a flat inside one of those ugly tower blocks, the sort of council-funded eyesores that only look good when they're a pile of rubble. Every time I go to one of these places, I lose the will to live, and not only that, I feel sorry for the people stuck here. It's bleak. The buzzers are always broken. Lifts broken. The smell of piss, shit and weed everywhere. Not to mention, it's always freezing cold inside. Always. I can only imagine how cold it is in the flats themselves. No wonder so many people are out of their faces on drugs around here. Might be the only way to keep warm and block out the smell.

I tell myself that this will be a flying visit.

I park next to a playground that's encircled by a chain-link fence. From there, it's a short walk to the main door, and as expected, the buzzer is broken. I'm about to send a message to the customer, hoping they'll come down and take the bag off me, when I try the door and realise it isn't locked.

Of course. *Just hurry up, Angie.* I don't use the lift (too many horror stories) and instead walk the stairs up to the fourth floor. It's exercise, if nothing else. At least the corridors are brightly lit, which is something to be grateful for. I move quickly, drop off the food at the customer's door, take a photo and walk back downstairs.

I exit through the broken door. The night feels like it's sharpening its claws, the air getting colder by the minute. I try to close the door properly, but the lock won't catch. Not my problem.

I hurry away from the tower block, past the playground and towards the Corolla. I'm crossing the road and on the brink of notifying the customer that their order has arrived when my hand goes over my mouth. Almost a minute passes before the initial shock wears off and I decide to trust my eyes.

"You've got to be kidding."

There's spray paint all over the passenger side of my car. It's hard to tell in the dark, but it looks like it's a mixture of bright orange and pink. No discernible shapes, words or patterns that I can make out. Just a swirl of mad, frenzied colour. The tyres have been slashed too.

What was that?

Did I hear laughter?

I look to the left, right and behind me. My eyes search for the faintest hint of movement. My ears prick up, listening for that laughter again or the sound of pitter-patter footsteps retreating into the night. Or worse, coming closer.

There's no one in sight. My mind is playing tricks on me, yet it feels like there are hundreds of pairs of eyes watching me at this very moment. This is a rough area, and it'd be unwise to forget it. Bad things happen around here.

"Shit," I whisper, suddenly feeling exposed.

I smash out a quick lap of the car, and there's paint splattered all over the driver's side too. All four tyres slashed. I'm not going anywhere.

Something whistles at my back. I glance over my shoulder, half expecting to see someone standing within arm's reach. A grinning face. Grabbing arms.

There's no one there.

I unlock the car, get in and slam the door shut. Then I make sure everything is locked. The Corolla isn't much of a refuge, especially when it can't go anywhere.

My phone chirps, and a fresh order comes in. I reject it and call Dan. All the while, I keep my eyes on the street. Front, back and sides. My hands are shaking, and it's not from the bitter cold.

"Hey," Dan says, picking up quickly. "Everything okay?"

"Hi. Are you home?"

"Yep. We got a lot done, and Richard was feeling generous. Got away about half an hour early."

"Right."

There's a short pause. Feels like I've got a knot in my tongue.

"Angie? Is something wrong? Or are you just skiving at work?"

"Definitely not skiving."

"What's up?"

I let out a long exhale, killing silence while my mind searches for the right words. There's no easy way to do this. "Listen, Dan. Something's happened."

His tone shifts from playful to concerned. "What? Are you okay?"

"I'm fine," I say quickly. It's far from the truth, but I have to reassure him that I'm not a bloody mess calling from the side of the road after a major car crash. "I just came back to the car after dropping off an order. It's been vandalised. The passenger side is covered in spray paint. All the tyres have been slashed too."

"Shit. Are you safe?"

"Think so. I mean yes. I'm sitting in the car."

"You've locked the doors?"

"Done."

"Okay," Dan says. I hear a frenzy of activity down the line. His feet thumping off the floor like he's running up and down the house. I hear Brogan bark, and long for the warm comfort of home. "I'm on my way. Drop me a pin for the address, will you? I'll be on the move in less than two minutes."

"Will do. Thanks."

"Fucking kids," he says. It's rare that Dan loses it, but I can hear the emotion in his voice. The anger. "Why did they have to slash your tyres too? Wasn't the spray paint enough?"

I tighten my grip on the steering wheel. "I don't think it was the locals."

"What are you talking about?"

Oh boy. This could be a mistake. "Well, it might have been but—"

"But what, Ang?"

"I think it's Martha."

The call goes silent. No breathing. No words. No footsteps rushing around the house in a frantic bid to find the car keys.

"Dan? Are you there?"

I hear him breathing in my ear again.

"What did you just say? Did you say ... *Martha? As in Martha Hunt?*"

"Listen, Dan. I haven't told you everything that's been happening lately."

"I don't like the sound of this."

I wonder if anything Dan is imagining right now is as bad as the real thing.

"Strange things have been happening to me since we fired her," I say. "One minute, I think it's November fifteenth messing with my head and making me blow little things up into big things. Then I'm convinced it's Martha Hunt messing with me. Because if she's the one who took my photo album and read the things I wrote about my childhood, she knows I'm a basket case at this time of year."

Silence follows. I can almost hear the wheels turning in Dan's mind.

"I don't understand," he says.

"I get it. This is a lot."

There's something like a soft groan in my ear. "I don't understand, Ang. What's going on here? Are you saying that Martha spray-painted your car and slashed your tyres?"

"Like I say, I don't have proof. But I think she's been harassing me."

"Why didn't you tell me?"

"I don't know," I say. "Because I didn't want to worry you. Because I kept thinking it would stop. And because you know what it's like at this time of year. I do get kind of worked up about things."

"So you didn't actually see her do anything?" Dan asks.

"No."

"Bloody hell," Dan says. I can picture him in the house, standing at the front door with his fingers on the handle.

Frozen to the spot. He's like a statue when he's processing information. "This is crazy."

"It's not just tonight," I say. "I'm having a weird old time lately. And everything weird that's happening, it all goes back to the day we kicked Martha Hunt out of our house."

Dan talks slowly. I know he's still trying to process, but now that I've opened the floodgates, I'm ready to talk. I don't even think about the fact that I'm holding him up. Delaying his departure and my rescue.

"Like what, Ang?"

"Something happened in George Square after the therapy session the other night. I was walking back to the train station when someone shoved me from behind."

"Someone shoved you?"

"Yep, next to the cenotaph. And I didn't see who did it. I went down, and whoever it was, they ran away."

"Oh fuck."

Dan only swears when he's really stressed. I'm the potty mouth in the family.

"Could be someone just bumped into you? Took off because they … well, because they're an arsehole."

"I think she's been in the house."

"Are you serious?" Dan asks.

"Yep, I'm serious. I think she's been in the house while we were out and possibly when I've been working at home during the day."

I think I hear him gasp.

"What makes you say that?"

"I sometimes get the feeling … the floorboards, you know? Except it's not quite the floorboards."

"They're loud. And the walls groan."

"I called the police."

His voice shoots up an octave. "What?"

"I thought she was in the house, Dan. She *might* have been in the house, but the police weren't exactly helpful."

I wonder if I'm starting to sound like a crazy person. Is that what Dan thinks? Is all this just gibberish?

"Why weren't they helpful?"

"They thought I was wasting their time."

"Because there was no one there?" Dan asks.

I sigh. "There was no one there. At least not by the time the police showed up."

"Bloody hell, Ang."

"Dan," I say, trying to force a blast of confidence into my voice, "that harmless-old-lady thing is just an act. She fooled us both. Martha Hunt is seriously unhinged."

"What else has happened?"

"I got a complaint at work about something that never happened. Had to talk to a rep. Looks like she's trying to get *me* fired now."

I decide not to tell him that Billie Jean went missing for a day. About the car speeding down the street minutes after she showed up. I think he'll be pissed off that I didn't call him earlier, and right now, I need Dan on my side.

"Let's say you're right," Dan says. "And she's responsible for all this. Why is she coming after you? Just because we fired her?"

"I don't know," I say. "Or maybe because I rejected her as a friend. You saw how strong she was coming on while we were on the road. All those texts. Texts with love hearts!"

"Oh, man."

"Well, she's not bothering *you*," I say. "Is she? And you fired her too."

Dan says nothing. I'm dumping a lot of stuff on him,

which wouldn't have happened if I'd been straight with him from the start.

"It's just all these things strung so closely together, you know? Things are moving in the house. Socks shoved to the wrong side of the drawer. Stuff that most people wouldn't notice, but I *do* notice."

Oh God. I sound like a madwoman.

"You're not crazy," Dan says, as if reading my mind. "Let me get this straight. Are you suggesting that Martha got a key cut?"

"Maybe." My voice cracks a little. "But I haven't seen her since we fired her. I've got zero proof."

"It's *not* you, Ang."

I hear the jangle of keys down the line. He's either at the door or already in the car. "We need to call the police. I'll do it on my way over there."

I hear the front door opening. Dan's voice directed elsewhere.

"Brogan, you stay in. There's a good boy. I won't be long – I'm going to get Mummy."

The door slams shut. I hear the scratchy sound of the key turning in the lock and then Dan's frantic footsteps as he hurries towards the car.

"Did you hear me, Ang? I said we need to call the police."

"No."

"No?"

"I don't want to get the police involved. At least, not yet. Not while there's a chance we can sort it out ourselves."

"Why not?"

"Dan, I'm serious. No police."

"C'mon, Angie. They'll believe us if—"

"If a man talks to them instead of a hysterical woman?"

He pauses. "I didn't say that."

I can't hide the irritation in my voice. "You didn't have to."

"Ang—"

"Dan, it was humiliating. I know it's hard for you to understand, but you weren't there, and you didn't see the way they looked at me. They made me feel like I was the criminal when all I did was ask for help. I don't want to call the police."

"It's the best option," Dan insists.

"Are you listening to me? We can't call them. I have no evidence against Martha. Nothing. To them, I'm just someone who freaks out when the floorboards creak. No police. Not until we have no other choice."

Dan exhales, a scratchy gust of wind in my ear. "Okay."

"You believe me," I say. "Don't you?"

"I believe you."

"Can you just get here, please?"

"Already on my way," Dan says. I hear the car door shut in my ear. The engine firing up and the crunch of tyres on gravel as Dan reverses out of the driveway.

"Give me twenty minutes," he says. "Whatever else you do, stay in the car, okay? Keep the doors locked and don't get out for anyone."

"I won't."

I WAIT IN THE CAR.

At least it's not a Saturday night, I tell myself. *That's something to be grateful for.* Things wouldn't be so quiet around these parts if it were the weekend, not with a pub located around the corner from the tower block. And it's a dive, too. A real shithole. There'd probably be an endless procession of pissed-up locals curious about the woman sitting alone in a vandalised car. Tonight there's only a couple of older men walking past and paying no attention to me or the car. Maybe spray-painted cars with slashed tyres aren't a rarity around these parts.

Dan is right about calling the police. I know it's the right thing to do, and that's what anyone else with their head screwed on would do in these circumstances. But I'm still hanging on to the thought of waiting her out. Hoping that she'll get bored. Is it really because I'm scared of what the police will think of me? Or is it because I'm not willing to admit to myself what Martha might be capable of?

At least we can change the locks now that Dan knows. That's something.

There's a sudden noise behind me. I breathe a sigh of relief as a purring engine signals Dan's arrival. A pair of headlights dazzles me in the rear-view. The car pulls up close behind me. Closer.

That's a little too close, Dan, I think.

I sit bolt upright in the driver's seat. Sucking in my stomach muscles, clenching tight fists at my sides. I look in the rear-view, then over my shoulder, wincing at the light that stabs my eyes. That's not Dan's car.

That's a silver Corsa.

A flood of terror pierces my brain.

Oh no. No, no, no.

The night is silent except for the car engine behind me. My eyes are locked on the mirror, but I can't see into the driver's seat. The headlights are too bright. I try to blink out the light and get a look at who's behind the wheel. My breathing is shallow and quick. Who am I kidding? I don't need to see who's behind the wheel. I know.

We sit here in a silent stalemate that seems to take place outside space and time, and all the while, a single thought rushes through my mind.

My car has no tyres. I can't get away.

CHAPTER FOURTEEN

Where are you, Dan?

The Corsa sits behind me, the engine idling. Nothing happens, and it's the wait that's killing me. I'd braced myself for impact, thinking that she was going to nudge me with her car. Nudge or something worse. But there's only this endless silence. And it's every bit as jarring as if she'd rammed the bumper of the Corsa into the back of my car.

"Leave me alone," I say, watching the lights in the mirror.

The street is poorly lit. The whole neighbourhood is poorly lit. It's hard to make out the silhouette of a person sitting in the driver's seat. At first glance, it looks like I'm being harassed by an angry, self-driving car.

I'm not losing my mind after all. She was in George Square, she was in the house, and she complained about me at work. The bitch even took my cat for a day. It was Martha all along, purposefully trying to drive me insane.

I grip my phone. I'd have called Dan, but he's on his way here anyway. What good will it do to call him? He'd only have a panic attack at the wheel. Floor it and put himself and others at risk. Anyone in their right mind would have called the police, but, even now, I can't bring myself to do it. There's this wall that goes up in my mind every time I think about involving the police.

Why is she just sitting in her car like that?

What's the right thing to do when there's a maniac at my back like this? Should I make the first move, get out of the car and confront her? That *is* her in the car, isn't it? Shit, even now I'm doubting myself. There's always room for a little more doubt. What if I've got it all wrong and it isn't Martha? It's possible. Someone in the tower block could've seen what had happened to the car, and now they've come down to help.

Bullshit.

My throat feels tight. I've got an invisible pair of hands around my neck, strangling me.

The metallic click of the driver's door opening sounds like a bomb. I flinch. Look in the mirror. Look over my shoulder. My heart pounds at the sight of a shadowy figure in the mirror. Still. Silent. Like a ghost.

I remain seated in the car, rigid from head to toe with terror. Even with the car seat underneath me, it feels like I'm falling into a deep hole.

"Dan, where are—"

She's out. She's standing beside her car. A round-shaped silhouette in the headlights, and I imagine her eyes burning with hatred. A skull-like grin on her face.

I'll take good care of things.

She raises her left arm, and I hear a noise. *Click-click. Click-click.* There's a bright flash of something a few inches above her head. The glint of metal in her hand, and each time she clicks, I see a tiny speck of orange blazing in the dark. Then it's gone; then it's back again.

Click-click.

I SIT *in the corner of the room while Jean, the therapist, talks to my aunt and uncle at the desk. They're lowering their voices, but I can still hear them. I'm sitting on a couch at the back of the room, looking down at the floor, sucking on the straw that's poking out of the apple juice carton. This room always smells the same – of fruit. Strawberries. Raspberries. The fruity odour is the only nice thing about it.*

This always happens at the end of the session. Auntie Rose and Uncle Matt get the lowdown while I get a cold drink, and on the way home, we'll stop in at the bakery on High Street, and I can choose any cake I want. It'll be an Empire biscuit for sure today. I'm pretty sure they'd rather I wasn't in the room, but I'm not dumb, and they know it. No one wants to ask me to leave. This is about me. I have the right to at least stay in the room.

"It's been almost two years since her mum died," Jean says to my relatives. "And she's still having these vivid nightmares about the fire."

"The nightmares come and go," Uncle Matt says. "But her fear of fire – that's a constant. She's terrified of it. The faintest hint of it is enough to set her off."

Auntie Rose, wearing her Sunday church clothes for some reason, chimes in. Her soft, whispery voice is so like Mum's. "We can't have a fire in the house. We can't let her see a bonfire on Guy Fawkes Night. We don't keep matches or lighters in the house. Matt's working on giving up smoking, but in the meantime he keeps his cigarettes and matches in the car. Never in front of her."

"I'll stop soon," Uncle Matt says. I can only see the back of his head, but I know he's blushing from the colour of his neck. He's fair-skinned and blushes easily. "I've cut down and feel so much better for it. Wee Angie comes first. She always will."

Jean smiles. She leaves a lengthy pause before resuming the conversation.

"This will hopefully improve over the years," she says. "What I'd like to do is get Angie to open up a little more. She's still a closed book when it comes to talking about her feelings. Who can blame her, considering what she saw?"

"How can we help?" Uncle Matt asks.

Jean clasps her hands together. Her forehead wrinkles in concentration. "Now, I don't think she's going to talk explicitly about these things. But you said she enjoys writing?"

Auntie Rose nods. "She's very creative. Essays. Short stories. Even a little poetry. But yes, she doesn't write to show others."

"That's good," Jean says. "How about on the way home, you stop in at a newsagent and let her choose a couple of notepads and some pens and pencils. No pressure. No explicit instructions. She doesn't have to write anything if she doesn't want to, but you can let her know that she has an outlet, and it's there any time she needs it. She can write about whatever she wants, and no one else has to read it. Actually, I think it's best if no one does. It's her private place. It's where her feelings go."

"Will it help with how jumpy she is around fire?" Uncle Matt asks.

Jean gives a shrug. Then she looks straight at me through

the gap between my relatives' shoulders. She smiles, and I see a flicker of doubt in her eyes.

"It's worth a try."

I ROCK BACK and forth in the driver's seat, screaming for help. Convinced that I'm about to throw up. Convinced that she's going to trap me in the car and set it – *set me* – on fire.

"Martha!" I scream. "Stop!"

This is the power she has over me. She knows what I fear most of all. She's read the things I wrote and that I keep locked away in the album and that no one was ever meant to see without my permission. All the horrors that go back years to that day, to *that* day, and even now, the way I tense up whenever I look at a box of matches or hear the sound of a lighter being struck.

But she keeps going.

Click-click.

I'm so scared I can't make a run for it through the passenger-side door. My legs aren't playing ball, and I think I'd topple over before taking three steps. I've dropped my phone down the side of the seat. I can't see it. Can't reach it.

Click-click.

What's she doing? Martha is approaching the car slowly. Still flicking the lighter on and off. Darkness recedes from her face, and, at last, I can see her features clearly. Big glasses. Big hair. That's it. I know for sure that it is her, yet what comfort is that right now? Here she comes.

Click.

Her eyes don't blink. What's next? What's she going to do to me?

Click.

A car!

Dan.

Martha stops and is perfectly still, a dark shadow rooted to the spot. The lighter goes quiet, the flame disappears, and she turns her head to look back down the road. A distant vehicle takes a left turn and is coming our way. A set of headlights swells and throws its golden net over the dark neighbourhood. The engine roars. The driver is in a hurry.

She gives me one last, silent look.

I watch in the side mirror as Martha runs back to her car. She slams the door shut, then performs a hasty U-turn before speeding off in the opposite direction to the incoming car.

I sit behind the wheel. Light-headed, dizzy and fuzzy. From somewhere out there in the night, I can still hear it.

Click-click.

CHAPTER FIFTEEN

I don't tell Dan what happened after he arrives.

He checks me out, and I convince him that I'm alright. For that, I deserve an Oscar. He checks out the spray paint and slashed tyres, shaking his head in disbelief.

"This is insane."

Somehow, I'm able to get my shit together despite what happened, which, as time passes, feels more like a nightmare than something that actually took place.

Dan keeps pushing to call the police. I can't do that. I can't make an idiot of myself in front of officers who don't care or understand. What will they say when I tell them that a cardigan-wearing granny scared the shit out of me by flicking her lighter on and off?

It wasn't anything to do with local thugs. It was Martha with the big glasses, the perm and her silly waddle-run.

Dan accepts it, for now at least. Then he makes some calls, and we arrange for the car to be towed to a local garage. After that, we go straight home and sit down at the kitchen table. We're quiet for a while. Processing. Finally, Dan gets up, opens the fridge and puts a bottle of cold beer in front of me. He peels the lid off and urges me to drink, which I do. Then he boils the kettle to make himself some tea, and I'm not surprised when he starts talking about the police yet again. I knew it was coming.

The beer is so cold and good. I don't want to talk – I just want to sit, drink and think. I've got a lot of thinking to do.

"Let's hold off," I say.

"Angie—"

"I really think it's over," I say, avoiding eye contact so Dan doesn't see the lie on my face. My fingernail chips away at the label of the beer bottle.

"Over?"

"Yes. I'm sure of it."

"Seems like it's escalating to me," Dan says, pouring hot water from the kettle into his cup. He puts in some oat milk, stirs, then brings it over to the table and sits down opposite me. "And if it *is* escalating, what's she going to do next?"

I should tell him. *Well, she went on a rampage with a lighter, and I thought she was going to set the car on fire with me in it. I can't wait to see what happens next either.*

"One more incident," I say. "One more and we'll call the police. Deal?"

He sighs. "I'm worried about this, Ang. I'm worried about *you*. She's not coming after us. She's coming after you. She's fixated on you."

"I'll be okay."

His thumb orbits the rim of the cup. So far, he hasn't touched his tea.

"I don't know. This is insane. This shouldn't be happening because we fired a house sitter. We need to start thinking about getting a restraining order against her. I could call a solicitor first thing in the morning."

"C'mon," I say. "It won't come to that."

Dan opens his mouth to protest. He stops himself and gives me the weakest of nods. "I hope you're right."

I brave a smile.

"Yeah. Me too."

"Seriously, Angie, keep your wits about you. If you so much as catch a glimpse of Martha in your vicinity, that's it. I'm calling the police. I'll deal with them if you don't want to. Happy to do all the talking. And I'm calling a solicitor."

"I'll keep my eyes open," I say. "I promise."

Dan shakes his head, and it's obvious he's still trying to take it all in. It's understandable. He's only just found about Martha's crazy streak. "Fixing the car won't be cheap," he says. "Her insurance, that's if she's got any, should be paying for it and also for a rental so you can keep working."

"I know."

He nods, and there's defeat in the gesture. Dan seems to realise that, right now, I'm a million miles away from practical discussions about the police, restraining orders and who's going to pay for car repairs.

"Okay," he says, hands in the air. "I've made my point. Listen, I can easily Uber it to work and back until the Corolla is fixed. You can use my car for deliveries, okay?"

"Are you sure?"

"Absolutely. I know you'll go insane if you're stuck in here all day."

I smile. "Thanks."

"Love you," he says, blowing me a kiss.

I catch it.

"Love you too."

Dan takes his tea to the bedroom, and I tell him I'll be in soon. I'm grateful for the silence that comes after he's gone. Now I can think.

What I haven't told Dan is that I've got no intention of sitting around and waiting for Martha to make her next move. Something will happen, of that much I'm sure. Martha won't stop. I saw the look in her eyes tonight, and I know she hasn't had her fill. But as freaked out by all this as I am, I'm done waiting around for Martha to make all the decisions. She won't go away until she's caused real, lasting damage to my life. Or until she's ended it.

There is one other option, though.

I could make her go away.

But how?

I take a second beer out of the fridge, then move from the kitchen to the living room. There's only a small lamp on in the corner of the room. It's dark and cool in here. That's what I want. Mind and body are wide awake because I'd usually be out delivering at this time of night. Might as well do something useful.

I stretch out on the couch, pick up my phone and open the notes app. As Billie Jean curls up beside me, I jot down several ideas on how to take some of the power back from Martha. In the end, it all boils down to the same thing – knowledge and information. She knows so much about me, and, in fact, she's glimpsed my soul through my writings. But I know so little about her. That *has* to change.

This is scary. I don't know what the hell I'm doing, but I can't do nothing, not if I'm not willing to go to the police.

The first thing I have to do is find out where she lives.

I make another note. It's the first item on the list for tomorrow morning.

Call the housesitting agency.

I DRINK THREE BEERS, which helps me get a decent night's sleep. After getting up at the same time as Dan, I shower, have breakfast, and after he's gone to work in an Uber, I'm back on the couch, looking at the notes app on my phone.

Call the housesitting agency.

I make the call, and a woman's voice answers. She's so stilted that at first I think I've gotten through to some AI voicemail.

"HouseSittersWeTrust," she says. "Can I help you?"

I sit forward. There's a pen and notepad on the coffee table in front of me. A cup of black coffee and a plate of toast that I haven't touched.

"Hi. I'm calling about one of your registered house sitters."

"Yes."

"Well, excuse me. I don't think she's on your books anymore, but she was until very recently. She might have been laid off."

"What's the name?"

"Martha Hunt."

Just saying her name makes the hairs stand up on the back of my neck. There's an awkward silence that lingers down the line.

"Hello?" I say. "Are you there?"

"Oh yes. I'm here."

"Martha Hunt?"

"Uh-huh."

"You know who I'm talking about, then?"

Another long pause follows.

"May I ask what this is in regard to, please?"

I take a deep breath. "Yes, it's related to the formal complaint that I made about Martha. She let my husband and me down badly during a recent house sit. I sent you a batch of photos and a written report of the damage she caused. She basically trashed our house."

"Hmm."

"Are you aware of the incident?"

"Yes."

Okay. I was expecting a little more than *hmm* and *yes*. Then again, this isn't exactly the most prestigious housesitting company, is it? She can tart her voice up all she wants, but she's not fooling anyone. This is most people's third or fourth choice at best. Or it's the short-notice choice for the desperate. Like it was for Dan and me.

After making the original complaint and getting the first apology (which was fine), I received a second but rather flaccid apology via email and then nothing after that. I had to get in touch to remind them about the refund, but they didn't offer to pay for any of the cleaning. All in all, I got the impression they wanted it (and me) to go away quickly. Can't blame them, I suppose.

"So what is this about?" the woman asks for a second time. Her tone is sharper. Colder.

This was already a long shot. Now it feels more like a swing for the heavens.

"Well, I need to ask you for a favour."

"Hmm."

"I was wondering ... could you give me Martha Hunt's address, please?"

Her voice cuts my ears like a razor. "Excuse me? Her home address?"

"That's right."

"What for?"

This is the part that I don't want to go into great detail about, especially not on the phone. Especially with a complete stranger.

"I ... I just need to talk to her. About what happened. About certain things that have happened since she was at our house."

Too much. That's too much.

"I see," the woman says. "You understand I can't just hand out a former employee's address to anyone. Or an email address for that matter. Even if she's not with us anymore, that information is still confidential."

It's the slap in the face I was expecting.

"I understand that. But let's just say that Martha hasn't taken her dismissal well. There's been some, umm, harassment."

"I'm sorry to hear that," the woman says in a flat voice that means *I don't give a shit*. "But that's a matter for the police. Martha is no longer on our books and no longer associated with HouseSittersWeTrust. She's got nothing to do with us."

"You sent her to me."

"You chose her."

Bitch.

"Fair enough," I say. "But isn't it better for all if I don't involve the police? If I can bring this matter to a close without fuss?"

I can almost see this woman's face as she sits in her little office or reception space. Bored and indifferent. She's probably scrolling on her phone right now. Checking her Instagram.

"I'm sorry," she says. "Rules are rules. I can't give you Martha's address. Was there anything else I can help you with?"

"That woman is dangerous," I say. "I'm asking you for help. Can't you just bend the rules this one time? Please?"

"If you don't feel safe," she says, "I recommend you call the police. Now, was there anything else I can help you with this morning?"

I hang up.

I PACE THE KITCHEN. Boil the kettle for a cup of tea I don't want.

Not a great start. Did I really think they were going to hand over Martha's personal details just like that?

Yes, I did.

Okay, it's back to the drawing board. I need to find her address. Because the problem is that when it comes to Martha and me, she has all the power. She knows where I live. She knows about Dan and where he works, where I work, and best of all for her, she knows about my family history.

She has everything. I have nothing.

Think, Angie, think. What do I know about this woman? Not much except that until recently, she worked as a house sitter for a C-level organisation. I know she's got issues, and that's putting it mildly. And ... that's it. That's my arsenal, and in terms of fighting back or scaring off Martha, it's not much to go on.

I bring my laptop to the kitchen table, where the Wi-Fi is better. I pull back a chair, sit down and sip on a freshly made green tea with lemon. Every time I hear the floorboards creak, I feel my heart speeding up. Dan said he'd get on to someone about changing the locks today. That the landlord was cool with it.

That'll make me feel a little better.

I type Martha's name into Google along with a selection of keywords that I wrote down on a notepad. Specifically, local towns and villages along with search terms like *house sitter* and *pet sitter*. I add *reviews* too. If she's been working as a house sitter for a while, there must be some trace of her.

There's a sudden knock at the door.

I jump out of my chair so fast it's almost an out-of-body experience. I hurry over to the window. The postman sees me, grins and waves a small parcel in the air. I open the door, take the parcel off him with a smile and do my best to act like this guy hasn't just chopped a week off my life.

I drop the parcel at the door (it's for Dan anyway), return to the kitchen table, sit down and realise my legs are still shaking.

There are some matches in the search engine. Mostly, these are reviews from her former career as a house sitter – reviews that mention her by name. It's hard to believe, but I'm seeing a lot of *positive* reviews next to her name. I don't get it. These people obviously didn't come home early to find Martha sprawled out naked on their couch. They didn't see the dog puke or the dirty plates and takeaway boxes. Didn't notice their pets had gained weight.

I skim the mostly generic reviews. There's nothing of

interest here, and all the reviewers seem to be borrowing from the same template – *highly recommended, such a great person, she's the only one I'll ever trust with my babies*, and so on. Bullshit. Either these people were fooled, or the reviews are fake. I suspect the latter, and it's probably the company rather than Martha that's responsible. Hard to trust anyone on the internet these days.

I refine my previous search and this time add *motor home* to the keywords. Didn't she say something about a motor home on her first visit? It rings a bell. That her daughter lived in one or was a traveller or something like that? I can't remember the details off the top of my head, that's if she gave any. It's another long shot, and it's mostly the same results that come up on the first page. I read through the reviews again in excruciating detail because I don't want to miss anything. It's a tough ask. The false praise is sickening.

But one excerpt from a five-star review catches my eye.

> *Martha looked after our dog, Lewis. She was so nice and friendly and put us at ease right away. We got on well, and I loved chatting about her daughter, Claire, and the motor home in the Cumbernauld leisure village. Happy with how it went. Just a joy, and our pets were well looked after.*

It's less gushing than some of the other reviews, which means it might be genuine. And it's yielded a result. Cumbernauld. Claire. If this review is genuine, then I've just learned something big about Martha. Something I hope might be useful.

"Let's see how you like being stalked," I say.

I type *Cumbernauld* and *leisure village* into the search

engine. Bingo. Eden Leisure Village is a rural site located outside Glasgow that, according to their website, is used for glamping, outdoor weddings and also offers pitches for motor homes exploring the Central Scotland region.

It's something. It could be nothing.

I pour the rest of my tea down the sink. After that, I check on Billie Jean and Brogan (both sleeping), then take Dan's car key off the hook. It's only when I get to the car that I realise I haven't even got my shoes on.

———

EDEN LEISURE VILLAGE looks like fun.

The site is a fifteen-minute drive from the house, and despite the seriousness of my task, I leave the suburbs behind with pleasure. Except I haven't really left them behind; it just feels that way as I drive through the pristine greenery that overlooks the Summerhill fields. The village is stacked with glamping pods, huts and "glampervans". The terminology is new to me as someone with little to no interest in the whole camping thing. Never understood the appeal. Still, there's a nice chalet, as well as hot tubs and spa treatments.

I wouldn't mind visiting this place under different circumstances.

I park near the entrance. Walk towards reception, and once again, it feels like I'm hundreds of miles away from the nearest town. I guess that's the point – getting away without getting away. I enter a small, well-kept reception area, and a woman with a blonde pixie haircut greets me with a friendly smile. She's wearing a red fleece jacket zipped up to the neck. As I enter, she's typing something on her phone.

There's a scented candle on the counter, and the fragrance is strong. Smells like strawberry. Whatever it is, I like it.

"Good morning," she says, putting her phone down on the counter.

"Morning."

"Can I help you?"

Then it hits me. I've been so preoccupied with finding this place that I haven't thought about what I'm going to say. Or how I'm going to say it without sounding like a weirdo.

"I hope so," I say, following the words with an unexpected spurt of nervous laughter. "I'm looking for a woman called Claire. I think she might stay here on and off. The surname *might* be Hunt."

"Claire Hunt?" the woman asks.

"Yes. I think she has a motor home. Umm, maybe her mother stays with her sometimes?"

Everything coming out of my mouth sounds like a question even when it isn't. My words feel muddled as I try to arrange them in my mind, but it's even worse when I say them out loud. I expect a blank look in response to my gargled nonsense. To my surprise, the pixie-haired woman nods with what I interpret as a knowing smile.

"There's only one Claire I can think of. That is, one who I'd consider a regular around these parts."

"Her surname wouldn't be Hunt, would it?"

The woman gives a gentle shake of the head. A sad smile as if she feels the disappointment in me. "No, I'm sorry. It's Bishop. Claire Bishop."

I feel myself deflate like a burst beach ball.

"Bishop?"

"That's right."

"Okay. Does she come here alone?"

The woman shakes her head again. "Oh, no, Claire's not a guest. She works in the spa. That's what I mean when I say she's a regular."

"Ohhhh, right."

The more I learn, the more my one, extremely thin lead seems to slip away from me. I'm wary of asking any more questions and getting the final nail hammered into the coffin of my hope. The review, if it *was* genuine, was clear. Martha's daughter, Claire, is here in Eden Leisure Village, either full-time or as a regular visitor in a motor home. At least, that's the impression I got.

Why would someone write that? Does anything make sense here?

"Can I ask you something?"

The woman nods. "Of course."

"This is going to sound a bit strange. But do you know if Claire's mother is called Martha?"

"Oh, I don't know. Would you like to talk to her yourself?"

My ears prick up. "She's here? Right now?"

"Yes, of course," the woman says in a delightfully chipper tone of voice. "She just started work half an hour ago. Want me to give her a call and ask her to walk over?"

"I don't want to disturb her," I say, trying to be polite. Hoping it doesn't backfire. "And this, well, it might be nothing."

"It's not a problem. The spa's only a one-minute walk from here."

"Okay then. I'd really appreciate it. Thank you."

I have to talk to this Claire person. I have to at least cross off the possibility of this place having a connection with Martha. Even if it's nothing, that's something. Sort of. What

I really want is at least a hint of Martha's address or the general area she comes from. It never came up in our conversation, and even if it did, I doubt she would have told the truth. I'm not sure the woman is capable of telling the truth when it counts.

She knows where I live. I need to turn that back on her.

The receptionist points to a small wooden bench tucked in beside the door. There's a table next to it, covered in magazines with their edges curled over. Among them, *National Geographic* and *Woman's Weekly*. It reminds me of a dentist's waiting room.

"Have a seat," the woman says, "and I'll give Claire a call."

I point to the door. "I'll wait outside if that's okay. I could use the fresh air."

The woman gives me a cheerful thumbs-up. Then she picks up her phone off the counter, and it looks like she's writing a text. "No problem. She'll be down in a couple of minutes."

I give her a wave and push the door open. "You've been super helpful. Thanks."

Back outside, I wander down the main path that leads away from reception and further into the camping site. It's a sunny, crisp morning. There's a big-sounding dog barking from somewhere inside the campsite. As I walk, I prepare myself for disappointment. *Hope is dangerous*, I remind myself. Never more so than today.

A cluster of sparrows swoops back and forth above my head. I zip up my jacket to keep the cold off my neck.

"Hi – are you looking for me?"

I turn around and see a tall woman walking down the path towards me. She's wearing a Leisure Village zip-up top and leggings that cling to her slim, athletic figure. Her dyed blonde hair is tied back in a ponytail.

"Are you Claire?" I ask.

She points to the name badge on her top.

"That's me."

I smile. "Then I'm looking for you."

We shake hands and find ourselves walking back towards the reception building. At Claire's suggestion, we take the weight off our feet and sit down on the wooden chairs outside the front door. The shade is cold but pleasant.

After briefly introducing myself, I get straight to the point.

"Does the name Martha ring a bell?"

Claire smiles, showing a set of perfect Hollywood teeth. If she is Martha's daughter, she sure as hell didn't inherit the house sitter's vampire teeth. "I've met a lot of people in this line of work. New faces come and go every day."

"I think you'd remember Martha. She's … different."

The smile disappears. Claire's eyes narrow in concentration, or is it discomfort?

"Martha, you say. What does she look like?"

I think about Martha's face as she stood behind my car, flicking her lighter on and off. The dead eyes. No blinking *Well, she looks like a monster.*

Claire looks at me. She leans forward a few inches on her seat, as if to check me out closer. "Is everything okay?"

I nod, but it doesn't feel convincing. This is much harder than talking in therapy. In matters of Mum's death and of my feelings, I'm at least knowledgeable. This all feels like one gigantic stab in the dark.

"This woman I'm asking about … she's been giving me problems, and I need to find out where she lives."

Claire responds with a tight-lipped smile. "I'm sorry to hear that."

My head swirls with possibilities. Is this conversation going anywhere, or will it prove to be a dead end? I feel the weight of hope and crashing failure in the same moment. And if this approach fails, then that leads to the thought of Martha's next attack and what she'll do to me. All these thoughts come and go within seconds.

"What was the surname?" Claire asks.

"Sorry?"

"You said Martha, didn't you?"

"I did."

"And the surname?"

"Hunt."

Something happens in Claire's eyes. The expression on her face is like someone who's just woken up and remembered a nightmare. She seems to sink into her chair. Her haunted eyes drift across the sunlit village.

"You know her," I say. "Don't you?"

"Hunt?"

"Yes."

She swallows hard. "Describe her, would you?"

"Big perm, flowery cardigan and glasses. Looks like the sort of person who volunteers in a charity shop. All smiles, at first."

Claire's nodding. "Yeah, I guess I knew from the start you were talking about *that* Martha. It's been a long time since I've heard from her. When I knew her, she used the surname Hunter."

I feel my insides tingling with excitement. "Martha Hunter?"

Claire lets out a long sigh, and she continues to drown

into the chair, pulled under by some invisible weight that I've just put back on her shoulders. Then she sits forward, hands clasped together. I notice a dark titanium wedding band on her finger. She twirls it around as she talks. "Martha was a regular here for a while."

"She had a motor home?"

"No, nothing like that. Day visits. She came in for spa treatments and a massage here and there. I guess this was almost three years ago. You don't have to be a guest to use the facilities."

"How often did she come in?"

Claire continues to twirl the ring on her finger. There's an increasingly pained look on her face as she talks. "Once a week at first. Then twice a week. It was her little luxury, that's what she called it. A gift to herself."

"What was she like?" I ask.

"Lovely," Claire says, forced to squint her eyes as the morning sun pierces the clouds. The entire village is lit up further, and it's starting to look like something out of an old Disney movie. Some magical, sun-kissed landscape. "That is, lovely at first. After that, she became a bit full on."

"In what way?"

"She was determined to initiate a friendship between us. I was okay with that up to a point."

"Up to a point?"

Claire looks at me.

"Sorry," I say. "I know I'm asking a lot of questions."

"It's okay. I'm just … I haven't talked about this or even thought about it in a long time."

I wait for her continue.

"She came on strong, you know? Just pushed it and kept pushing the idea that we should hang around together. That we should become buddies. Every visit, it would always come up. Let's go out, Claire, you and me, let's get a drink and just hang out together, you know? Shoot the shit. It wasn't a sexual thing. I think she just wanted the company."

"You got lonely vibes off her?"

"I'm no expert," Claire says. "And I didn't get much out of Martha in terms of her personal history, but yeah, she's definitely a lonely person. There's something missing. Some gap that she's trying to fill."

"Gap?"

"Like, she fixates on things. I told her that I had bad acne as a teenager and that I'm still really sensitive about my skin. Paranoid about the tiniest little blemish, you know? What does Martha do? She starts bringing in all these products with her to every massage. Bags full of skincare products, creams and all this stuff. She must have been spending a fortune."

"Wow."

"Exactly."

"So you said no?" I ask. "To hanging around with her?"

"I should have," Claire says.

We exchange looks.

"Uh-oh," I say.

Claire nods. "Yep. I mean, it was okay at first. We went to a tea house not far from here and had some cake and a nice little chat. It was ... *fine*. Like I said, I sensed she was lonely, and I thought I was doing a good thing, but I always knew—"

She hesitates.

"That something was off about her."

I wonder if she knows the half of it, I think.

"Did you guys hang out more than once?" I ask.

Claire makes a face like she's tasted something bitter on the end of her tongue. "I went to her house."

It doesn't sink in at first. What I just heard. Then I get the soft tickly feeling of a spider crawling down the back of my neck. A big one. I leap forward on my seat.

"You've been to her house?"

"I have."

"Where does she live?"

Claire is playing with her wedding ring again. Twirling it faster than ever. "Behind that massive discount supermarket in Bishopbriggs. There's stretch of woodland at the back with a clearing and a caravan site on it. They're kind of hidden away – not nice but cheap to rent, I imagine."

"Martha lives on a caravan site?"

"She did three years ago."

"What happened when you went there?"

Claire's nervous smile is an answer of sorts. "That was the day I found out she was making plans for us to go on holiday together that summer."

"Yikes."

"Yeah. She was so excited. Talking like we were students about to go on a gap-year adventure. She'd done her research on accommodation and things to do. And she kept banging on about Spain, Italy, Scandinavia. There were travel brochures lying around everywhere. Pamphlets. Maps. It was unnerving."

"How did you get out of it?" I ask.

"I panicked. Said the first lie that leapt to mind, that I was scheduled to go to South Africa for a couple of months in the summer. That I was due to spend some time with my uncle Hugh in Cape Town."

Claire laughs while shaking her head.

"To this day, I have no idea where it came from. It was all nonsense. Just something that I blurted out in a panic."

"Do you have an uncle Hugh?"

"Both my parents are only children."

I smile.

"How did it play out?"

"Not good. I tried to keep my distance after that. Played it cool and stuck to the story that I was going to South Africa every time she came to the spa. I was hoping if I cooled off the friendship, Martha would stop coming here. And she did. For a while."

"A while?"

"She came back with a vengeance in the summer. She bypassed reception that morning and stormed into the spa only to see me here when I was supposed to be in Cape Town. Turns out Martha doesn't like rejection."

"Oh God." *No shit, Sherlock*, I think.

Claire shivers and pulls her zip up to her neck. Shoves her hands in her pockets. If we were in a bar, I'd be ordering her a stiff drink.

"It was horrible. Martha started yelling and screaming. She didn't even build up to it, she just went batshit crazy. Thank God there were no other customers in the spa at the time. She charged over to the counter, picked up this ornate candleholder and chased me into the back. Literally chased me, swearing and calling me all sorts of names. It would've been funny if it weren't so terrifying."

"I'll bet," I say.

"It was the look on her face," Claire says. "She was gone. I mean *gone*. To this day, I don't know what would've happened if she'd caught me."

Claire looks at me.

"And she was saying all this horrible stuff about my skin. About my acne. About cutting me up and scarring me for life and how no poxy cream would ever help."

"That's vicious." I hold her gaze. "How did you get away?"

"One of my assistants called the police, but Martha had left by the time they arrived. After that, I never saw her again. Guess I got lucky. Well, I *know* I got lucky."

Claire lets out a long exhale, and her chest sinks. She sits up straight in the chair, shaking out her arms a little, flicking her wrists. Shaking out the memories.

"How did you find me, Angie?"

"It's complicated."

"Oh?"

"Martha's been working as a house sitter. I found your name in a glowing online review for her services."

Her eyes widen. "My name?"

"She's been telling people that you're her daughter. That you guys sometimes live together in a motor home here in the leisure village."

"That's insane," Claire says, her face pale in the sun. "Why would she do that?"

"Good question."

"I was kind of hoping that Martha had forgotten all about me."

I nod. "Don't worry. Her fixation has moved on."

Claire hesitates. "You?"

"Yep."

"Oh no. I'm sorry. Have you called the police?"

"Umm, sort of. I'm kind of hoping to nip it in the bud before it gets into legal territory. Now I know where she lives."

"And then what? What will you do when you've found her?"

I shrug, tell Claire the truth. "Don't know."

We stand up, replace the chairs where we found them and walk back onto the winding path that leads away from reception and into the village. The sky above is hazy with clouds, but there's still plenty of late morning sunlight shining down.

We stop walking, and Claire turns to face me.

"She's dangerous, Angie," she says. "You should call the police and let them deal with it. I'll never forget the look on her face when she was chasing me with that candleholder. *Gone*. I swear to God, I thought she'd—"

She shakes her head.

"Never mind."

Claire whistles under her breath, then looks down at her shoes. There's a lightness about her again, but it feels forced for my benefit.

"Well, I'd better get back to work."

"Of course. Thanks a lot for this. If I can just ask one more—"

"Number seven," she says so quietly that I almost miss it. And then she begins to walk away up the path, back towards the spa.

"Hmm?"

She stops. Turns around.

"Martha. She lives in caravan seven."

CHAPTER SIXTEEN

I'm in the supermarket car park. Sitting in Dan's car, working up the courage to get out and go find Martha's caravan.

The supermarket is an ugly block of contemporary architecture, about a mile south of the town centre in Bishopbriggs. There's a fenced-off yard at the back and, behind that, a shrinking area of woodland. Somewhere in the woods is a clearing with twelve caravans. The dingy old caravan park is an anomaly in an affluent and expanding suburb like Bishopbriggs. Sooner or later, the land will be bought and paved over. The woods will disappear, and houses or flats will be built. Shops, maybe.

I hope Martha still lives in the caravan. Claire said it's been around three years since she came here.

I'm scared out of my mind. Scared shitless. The thought of walking up to Martha's front door and knocking is the stuff of nightmares. I'm not a hero or some kind of whizz private detective who's good at the dangerous stuff. The reason I'm here is that I want it all to go away. But it won't.

Doing nothing is unthinkable.

And despite Martha's craziness, there's still a part of me that wants to believe we can talk this thing out like mature adults. Call me a dreamer.

I drink some water. Open the car door and get out. It's a chilly afternoon in the north of Glasgow, still cloudy but bright. I zip my jacket up as far as it will go. Blow out a fine mist of breath as I summon up the courage to start walking. Looks like the primary schools are out judging by the number of parents I see walking their tiny, uniformed kids alongside the main road. Some of them veer off towards the supermarket entrance.

I glance at my reflection in the car window. My hair is tied back. My skin looks paler than usual.

"What am I doing?" I ask, but my reflection has no answer.

I walk over a narrow strip of grass, the sound of little children laughing in my ears. The grass leads to a short but steep climb that leads away from the supermarket car park and onto the pavement. There's a dirt track behind the supermarket. That's where I'm heading. From the start of the track, it's a two- or three-minute walk into the woods, and then, if I remember correctly, it'll take the same time to reach the clearing with the caravan site.

My legs begin to shake on the dirt track. Palms sweaty. I ignore the pleas in my head to turn around, relent to Dan and Claire's advice and call the police.

I keep walking.

The traffic sound of the main road fades to a whisper. A mob of stooped trees lines the track and blocks out the sun. It feels like I'm in a dark fairy tale, the naked limbs of the trees reaching for me with bad intentions. I'm delighted to see a dogwalker with an off-leash Staffy. The man says hello, and then he's gone. I keep forcing myself forward. It's not the most pleasant of routes to walk. There are bald, dried-out patches of earth at the edge of the track. The path is lumpy, and there's no shortage of litter – Coke cans, cigarette packets and plastic containers that once held sandwiches.

The clearing is still there and so is the caravan park. It's tucked in to the right-hand side of the track. It's not a welcoming sight, and it feels like something forgotten, something that no longer belongs in the town. The clearing is smaller than I remember from whenever I passed this place years ago. Didn't give it a second glance back then. The old, beat-up caravans are cramped together. There's a second dirt track on the opposite side, not as well kept as the one I'm on, and most likely it leads to a road that lets cars get in and out.

I can imagine parents telling their children to steer well clear of this place. There are a few cars and one white van parked on-site, taking up space along with some battered-looking outdoor furniture. There's a pair of ripped jeans and a Santana T-shirt hanging on a washing line.

I don't see a Corsa. Maybe she parks it in town. Or maybe she doesn't live here anymore.

A dog barks as I approach. There's a whiff of stale cigarette smoke hanging in the air.

What if she has a dog? Never thought of that, did you?

This is a terrible idea. A surge of panic rises in my throat, and my legs feel like hollow stumps. I scold myself for having nothing but a vague plan about catching Martha off guard and hoping it'll rattle her enough to leave me alone. She's a complete psycho, and here I am, thinking that I'm some kind of hero in an old-fashioned western.

I could leave. I *should* leave.

All the caravans have numbers painted on either the back or side. It doesn't take me long to find what I'm looking for.

Number seven.

It's a battered, crusty-looking caravan. It's probably been sitting in the same spot for decades, its travelling days long gone, the pink and white exterior succumbing to the elements. I see two windows at the front, both covered with grubby lace curtains. I climb the steps that lead to the door and get a whiff of gas or rotten eggs.

What the hell is about to happen here?

I don't hear anything through the door. No TV, no voices. I glance over my shoulder to see if anyone else is watching me. The owner of that big-sounding dog, for example. Can't see anyone. There's not much sign of life at all around here.

Let's get this over with, I think.

In a rush of movement, I knock, step back from the door and wait. My body is taut, ready to run, ready to fight. I hope it doesn't come to either one.

Silence.

I knock again. Louder this time.

There's no answer. Does she still live here? A lot can happen in three years, yet there's something about this worn-out caravan site that suits Martha to a tee. I knock harder, and there's still no answer. Tentatively, I approach the door. Pin my ear against it, listening for the faintest hint of sound. Anticipating the shudder of heavy footsteps on the floor.

Nothing. If Martha still lives here, she's not home.

It's a kick in the teeth, especially after plucking up the nerve to come here and do this. Now I'm going home, and as far as Martha's concerned, she's still in control. Will I have the guts to come back?

Sod it. I knock again, just in case she's passed out in there. Wouldn't surprise me if she was lying in bed, cradling a bottle of vodka or pills. Nothing would surprise me about Martha.

I'm met with complete silence.

I walk away from the caravan site, back onto the gravel path.

As I walk back to town, it feels like there's someone following me. I look back. Nothing. No one. I walk faster. I'm about ready to break into a run when I hear the sound of traffic up ahead, and it sounds like a chorus of angels singing in my ears. A car horn blares, the heavenly trumpet welcoming me back to civilisation.

I wipe the sweat off my forehead. There's cement hardening in my legs as I walk back towards the supermarket car park. I'm edging off the pavement and onto the grass when the sound of raised voices in the distance makes me stop.

I look over my shoulder.

Sure enough, there's some kind of disturbance. It's coming from a bus stop about fifty metres up the road.

I let out a gasp.

Martha is standing at the bus stop. She's having an argument with some guy on a motorbike who's pulled into the bus stop alongside her. The biker is huge – a silverback gorilla with a patch on the back of his sleeveless denim jacket. I inch closer in that direction and notice the pattern of his patch – a dog skull with wings sprouting out at the side. *Road Wolves* is printed under the design. The man's bike, could be a Harley for all I know, is black and chrome with high handlebars and a deep, distinctive rumble coming from the engine, which he switches off as he dismounts. I can only see some of his face, but he's almost as wide as he is tall. Long straggly hair, brown and grey. Goatee. Tattoos covering both arms.

Why's Martha yelling at an old biker?

I'm standing in the open. Even though I'm next to a busy road that's swarming with traffic and people, if Martha looks over here, there's a good chance she'll spot me. And I'm close to her nest. Can't imagine she'll react well to that. And clearly, she's not in a good mood.

Right now, she's too caught up in the argument with the biker to notice anyone else. Both of them are yelling full blast. They make theatrical arm gestures. They're in a bubble, seeing nothing else but the person in front of them.

Passers-by take a wide berth. Steering their kids and dogs well out of the way.

I linger at a set of nearby traffic lights, giving the impression of someone crossing the road. My eyes are locked on Martha and the biker. The argument is heating up. Martha's stabbing her fingers in the big guy's face. I can't make out any of the words they're saying, but they sure as hell aren't exchanging pleasantries.

After a few minutes, Martha storms away but not before turning back one more time to flick the big guy the middle finger. He shakes his head, and she waddles away, off the pavement and towards the dirt track.

She still lives there.

Do I go after her? That's what I should do, yet something holds me back. It's the sight of the biker climbing back into the saddle. Once there, he lifts his helmet off the handlebars, puts it over his head, and he's fastening the strap by the time

I decide to run over there. And I do run, like my life depends on it.

"Excuse me," I call out, coming to a stop on the pavement side. And when he either doesn't see me or ignores me, my hands are up, waving to attract his attention.

There's a flicker of curiosity in his eyes. His voice is gruff and muffled through the helmet.

"What is it?"

I point towards the dirt track.

"That woman you were talking to," I say, making an effort to raise my voice above the traffic. "Do you know her?"

"What woman?"

"The woman you were arguing with. The perm, the glasses. Martha."

The biker keeps looking at me like I'm something that just moved in a lab jar. "What's this about?"

"Please, it's important. Do you know her?"

There's a jolt of emotion. A single tear rolls down my cheek, and I don't know where it comes from. My voice cracks as I continue to talk.

"That woman is making my life hell. She's harassing me. Following me. I'm scared of what she'll do next."

His eyes soften. At least, I think they do. "Can't say I'm surprised."

"So you do know her?"

His laugh is sudden. It's so big that his entire body shudders on the bike like he's being electrocuted. While he laughs, the rest of the busy road fades into the background, and the biker expands in front of me like a mythical giant. A man mountain. Even sitting down, he towers over me.

"You seem like a nice girl, so I'll give you some advice. That woman? Stay away from her. She's dangerous."

"It's too late for that."

He sizes me up and shakes his head. "Stay away from her anyway. You're no match for her."

"You *do* know her?"

That earthquake laugh returns. "Know her? Fuck, I was married to her for twenty years."

He might as well have shoved me all the way back to my car.

"You were *married* to Martha?"

He shakes his head. "No."

I frown. "But you just said—"

"I never said I was married to Martha. I was married to that woman. I was married to her before she changed her name."

The biker glances down the busy road, which is still flowing with traffic. He points to a double decker that's due at this stop. The bus is waiting at traffic lights, but it'll be here in a minute.

"Bus coming. Better clear this space."

"Wait!" I yell. "What do you mean? What was her name before?"

He grips the handlebars and assesses the road as he prepares to join the flow of traffic.

"Stay away from her," he yells back. "That's all you need to know."

The bike roars as it merges onto the main road. A few moments later, the double decker bound for Glasgow city centre pulls into the space. The doors hiss open, and several passengers step off. I clear a path. When the bus drives off again, I'm the only one left at the stop, still staring at the road. Still processing what I just heard.

I can't go back to Martha's caravan. Not now. Not when she's in a foul mood.

More than that, though, I'm thinking about the name I saw on the biker's patch.

Road Wolves.

They sound a little ... scary? But I have to find them. If there's any chance I can find out who Martha really is, I *have* to find them.

CHAPTER SEVENTEEN

It's been a long day, and it isn't over yet.

At six o'clock that evening, I kiss Dan goodbye, and as far as he's concerned, I'm going out to work as normal. He's never particularly overjoyed to see me going out to deliver food through the night, but we've had that discussion several times. He knows that making my own money while I get my writing off the ground is important to me. Still, the whole Martha-coming-after-me thing is another reason for him to be nervous.

"Late one?" Dan asks after we kiss at the front door.

"Not sure."

He nods. "Maybe one of these days we'll get to spend a weeknight together?"

I glance at my little family – Dan, Brogan and Billie, all gathered around the hallway like it's an official send-off. "I'd like that."

Dan gives me a bonus hug, and he squeezes tighter than usual. "Take care, Ang. I mean that."

I wave before setting off towards the car.

"Always."

I DON'T GO to work. Instead, I drive to the headquarters or clubhouse (or whatever bikers call their den) of the Road Wolves Motorcycle Club. To my surprise, it wasn't hard to find the address online. The clubhouse is located in Partick, just off Dumbarton Road in the west end of the city. I follow the GPS and park in a nearby street, having decided to keep Dan's car out of sight. Mine is already stuck in the garage for repairs and a respray, and I don't want to have to report to Dan that his car is wrecked too.

It's a two-minute walk along Dumbarton Road from where I park. A left turn and I'm looking down at the Road Wolves clubhouse.

As with my visit to Martha's caravan, I've been battling with the voice of reason, and it's telling me to get out of there. *You're out of your depth, Angie.* I don't disagree, but I keep walking forward. The biker connection might be important. And I'm desperate.

It's not much to look at. The clubhouse is an old pub that was taken over and converted more than thirty years ago. It's at the end of a narrow road littered with potholes. Not a problem for bikes to plot a route through, but not so great for cars. Maybe that's the point? Streetlights are few and far between. I see the Wolves logo painted front and centre on the building, serving as both a warning and a welcome to potential visitors. I'd expected to see more motorbikes parked outside the building, but there's only one. There's a mangled BMX propped up against the wall. Looks like it's been there for years.

I hear thumping bass from inside, the sort of bottom end that lands like a punch to the stomach. Moody, high-pitched rock vocals.

Maybe I should text Dan. Let him know where I am in case something happens. On second thoughts, he'd probably have a heart attack. If not, he'd be furious with me for lying about going to work and instead coming to a place like this.

I walk up to the door, and the muffled music from inside gets more intense. There's no one at the door, yet I'd envisioned some kind of bouncer or security system. Maybe I've watched too many films. There's a small black globe in the top corner of the doorway. I think it's a camera. Looking closer, a red pinprick of light blinks on and off as if to confirm my guess. If someone's watching from inside, it's clear they don't consider me a threat.

Time to get this over with.

I pull the door open and walk inside. The music goes up tenfold and hits me like a sledgehammer to the face. Now I recognise it. AC/DC. "Thunderstruck". The smell of stale cigarette smoke is rampant. No smoking ban in here.

The clubhouse interior is impressive, especially considering the shabby exterior. The walls are painted bright red, and there's a giant Road Wolves banner hanging on one side of the main space and, on the other, an exhibition of framed posters from the gang's history – a mini museum of sorts. The bar is small, tucked into the far corner of the main room, with stools lined up along the counter. Wooden tables fill the centre of the room. There's also a vintage-looking motorbike in the corner near the door, just thrown in there, I assume, for ornamental or symbolic value.

Despite the loud music, it's quiet as far as people are concerned. There are a few long-haired men with beards who give off typical biker vibes, but there are plenty of well-groomed younger men in here too. A few women. It's more civilised than I was expecting, but, again, I watch too many films.

My entrance hasn't gone unnoticed. I get a few looks, but no one bothers me, for now. My plan is to get this done and dusted before my nerves give out.

I walk to the bar, intending to give a description of the man I'm looking for. I'm halfway there when I see him. He's not exactly hard to spot, given the size of him. He's a man mountain who stands out in a place with plenty of other big men. He's in a back room, separate from the main bar, playing pool with a gaunt, leathery-faced biker who looks like he's in his seventies. The giant biker leans over the table, cue in hand as he weighs up the next shot. His movement is graceful for such a big guy. He takes the shot, and there's a loud *crack* as the balls scatter across the felt.

He hasn't noticed me yet.

I walk towards the bar. The man behind the counter is wearing a black waistcoat with the grinning wolf skull logo on the breast. His arms are bare, exposing a lot of ink.

"Help you?" he asks.

It's an effort to make myself heard over the music.

"Am I allowed in here?"

"As long as you're buying a drink."

I nod. "Umm ... can I get a beer, please?"

"Any beer in particular?"

I look at him like he asked me to recite the alphabet backwards. "Anything. I don't mind."

He nods. "Don't mind it is, then. That all?"

I point a thumb over my shoulder towards the pool room. "Is it okay if I go over and talk to that man at the pool table?"

I'm not sure why I'm asking to go and talk to another adult like requesting permission is the done thing. I wouldn't do that in any old pub, but this isn't any old pub, and I get the feeling that the usual rules don't apply. It seems right to ask. Safer.

The barman touches his ear. "You'll need to speak up, darling."

"I want to talk to that man!"

He nods, indicating that the message is received. "What for?"

I lean over the bar, not wanting to shout so everyone in the room can hear me. "I spoke to him yesterday in Bishopbriggs. We didn't get a chance to finish our conversation."

The barman's eyes cut through me like a laser. "What's it about?"

Bloody hell. Do I have to tell the barman my life story in order to talk to someone else? I kind of hoped he'd just say, *Aye, on you go. Help yourself. Here's your change.*

"His ex-wife."

The AC/DC song finishes at the exact moment I speak. I expect all heads to turn in my direction, but after an eternity of silence (it's about three seconds), another rock anthem comes on, and I've never been more thankful to hear Judas Priest in all my life.

The barman is still giving me the hard stare.

"His ex?"

I nod.

Meanwhile, an older biker with straggly grey hair sitting on a nearby barstool turns in my direction. He gives me a hard look. *Oh shit.* My legs are like jelly. This doesn't feel like a safe space for a woman on her own to expose weakness.

"Why are you interested in his ex-wife?" the barman asks.

A gruff voice cuts in from behind.

"It's alright, JJ."

I turn back to see the big biker standing in front of me like he materialised out of thin air. Pool cue in hand, holding it like a spear at his side. He looks the same as yesterday, all denims, greasy hair and tattoos.

"I met this young lady yesterday in Bishopbriggs. Looks like she's gone to some trouble to find me."

I feel myself blushing.

He gestures towards the pool room.

"Do you play?"

My voice comes out thin. "I used to."

"Well, I don't do sit-down interviews, and I assume that's why you're here. For an interview?"

I shrug. "I mean … a conversation would be better."

He grins at me. "Pool it is, then."

I take my drink and follow him across the room, weaving our way past the tables and into the pool room, where it's a little quieter. The air feels cooler too, which is nice. I grip the beer bottle, taking frequent sips for courage. Big biker grabs the triangular rack and sets the table for a new game. I've got no idea where his friend is.

I take a cue from the stand and chalk the tip. It's been years since I played pool, and I wasn't much use back then.

"You wanna break?" he growls.

"You go ahead."

"Age before beauty," he says. Then he breaks, hammering the white ball into the colours and scattering them across the table.

He studies the balls, gives a half-hearted shrug.

"What's your name?" he asks.

"Angie."

I inch my way around the table. Without too much thought, I take a shot and pot a red in the bottom corner pocket. The biker gives a wry smile; he's probably wondering if I'm a hustler. Only we aren't playing for money. At least, I hope not.

"And you?"

"William."

I miss the follow-up red. "Your shot, William."

He walks around the table like a soldier studying a model battlefield. "I'm impressed, by the way."

I frown. "Because I potted a ball?"

His deep laughter makes the walls shudder. "No. Because you found me."

"It's not that hard to find out where the Road Wolves hang out."

Another shrug of those massive shoulders. "No, I suppose not. You saw my patch, went on the internet and tracked me down. Still, it took guts walking in here. You don't make a habit of walking into biker clubs all alone, do you, Angie?"

"No."

"Good. Because they're not all as welcoming as we are."

"I'll keep that in mind."

William lowers his cue onto the rack beside the wall. Then he walks back to the table. His gnarled hand rests on the surface, two fingers drumming the green felt. "What do you want, Angie?"

"I want to know who Martha is," I tell him. "I want to know who she *really* is. The woman who's making my life hell."

His face is a grim mask of reluctance. The voice, heavy and tired. "And what will you do with that information?"

"Whatever I have to."

"Have you tried calling the police?"

"I didn't expect to hear that sort of talk here."

"Have you?"

"It's complicated."

William sighs. "Okay then. How much do you want to know?"

"All of it."

"In that case," he says, "you'd better tell me what she's done."

I tell William everything that's happened since we hired Martha to house sit. I talk like I'm at a therapy session, no holding back. I explain that ever since we fired her, she's been making my life a misery. I tell him about her forcing friendship on Claire from the Eden Leisure Village. That she's homed in on me now and, so far, hasn't bothered with Dan.

William listens without a single interruption. I see the shadow of discomfort flaring up in his eyes and a tight-lipped grimace. He nods when I'm finished.

"Aye. Let's just say she's developed a ... *sensitivity* ... to rejection over the years."

I finish the rest of my beer and put the empty onto a small table next to the couch. Beside an ashtray overflowing with cigarette butts.

"I'd like to know more about her," I say.

There's a wariness in his eyes as he drops down onto the couch, his broad shoulders sagging under an invisible weight. I think of Atlas holding the celestial spheres on his shoulders at the command of Zeus. Right now, William's burden seems heavier.

"Where do I even begin?" he says.

"How about with her name?"

"I talk better with a beer in hand, Angie."

I hurry back to the bar and buy William a beer. I'd love another one for myself, but I'm driving, so I settle for a Coke with ice. Besides, I want to be clear-headed because I think William, as painful as it might be for him, is about to give me that crucial information that could make the difference. Or maybe I'm expecting too much. Either way, it's better than waiting for Martha to strike.

Back in the pool room, we resume the conversation.

"Well, she's not Martha Hunt," he says, repeating what I learned yesterday. "That's just something she made up later on. Her real name is Rita Morrison."

"Are you still married?" I ask.

"Dear God, no. Are all your questions this good?"

"Sorry."

William smiles, and I don't see a big scary biker in front of me anymore – just a tired old man who'd rather be doing anything else than answering my questions. And yet here he is. He could get up and leave. Better still, he could get me thrown out. But he's here. Talking.

"What's her story?" I ask, leaning against the pool table and facing William on the couch. That game of pool we started is long forgotten. "Why is she pretending to be someone else?"

William takes a slug of cold beer. "She's not pretending to be someone else," he says, shaking his head. "She's still the same mad Rita I knew before. It's just that now she's mad Martha."

"Was she a part of this club?"

"The Road Wolves?"

I nod.

"Aye," William answers. "She was here at the beginning, just like I was. First at the old headquarters in Springburn and then later here."

He smiles, and it takes years off his face.

"Rita and I go way back. Not quite childhood sweethearts, more like teenage lovebirds. Lust at first sight. Oh boy, she was … *something*. Untameable. Forget that cardigan and the stupid fucking haircut and those ridiculous glasses. It's a disguise, nothing but a disguise. She's still Rita underneath all that shite."

He laughs, his eyes staring into empty space.

"She was fierce. Didn't take any shit off people, you know? Even when she was young. I liked the ferocity – at first."

"When did you get married?" I ask.

There's a hint of mournfulness in his voice.

"A lifetime ago. She was nineteen. I was twenty-one. We were both too young, too stupid, and our parents had long since written us off as lost causes. We got married about the same time as the Road Wolves were starting out, you know? Turned out to be one hell of a biker wedding. That was a good day."

He closes his eyes. Goes back to some place that puts a contented smile on his face.

I'm still trying to process the thought of Martha as a biker chick while listening to what William has to say. Even after all the crazy shit she's done so far, it was hard to think of Martha sitting on a Harley. But as William said – she's not Martha. She's Rita.

"Do you have any children?" I ask.

"Boy," William says, opening his eyes again. "Well, he's a man now."

"How old?"

"Ohhh, he's almost forty. I forget."

I sip my Coke, and it gives me brain freeze.

"That was quite a look I got from the barman," I tell William, "when I said I wanted to talk to you about your ex-wife."

"Aye." William wipes beer froth off his beard with his sleeve. "It's kind of a sore point around here."

"How sore?"

"Very sore."

I don't say anything because I sense William isn't finished. Sure enough, he gets up and closes the door. The hard rock music from the bar becomes muffled background noise. Then he goes back to the couch and picks up where he left off.

"We were going through a rough patch," he says, his gravelly voice much easier to hear now. "This was over twenty years ago. We were twenty years married before that, and we've almost been twenty years divorced."

"What happened?"

"Same thing that happens to so many marriages. The electricity fizzled out, and we realised there wasn't much of a friendship to fall back on. And we were both, well, seeing other people, if you know what I mean. Nothing long term."

"Was it an open marriage?" I ask.

"Nah, nothing as modern as that. But I made the mistake of flirting with Rita's best friend, Sadie. Stupid, but I'd always had a thing for her, and as it turned out, the feeling was mutual. She was unattached at the time. One thing led to another, as they say. Rita was never supposed to find out, but she did. And it didn't end well."

"You said it. She doesn't like rejection."

William's smile is heavy. "Aye."

"What happened?"

"Rita and a knife. That's what happened."

I gasp. "Did she—?"

"Kill Sadie? No, but she might as well have. Rita paid her a visit in the middle of the night. She had a spare key. Let herself in, caught Sadie by surprise and cut her up. Not just a little, you understand? Cut her bad. Her face."

He closes his eyes again. Shakes his head, lost in some terrible recollection.

"Oh my God," I say. "That's awful."

I feel the chilling sensation of icy-cold fingers pulling at my flesh. At the same time, I think about Martha chasing Sadie around the spa with a candleholder.

"Sadie never got over it," William says. "The scars on her face faded a bit. The ones in her head? Not so good. She locked herself away from the world and, even now, hardly ever sets foot outside. She's what you'd call a recluse, I suppose. Nervous and skittery as a deer in the headlights. I think she has a heart attack every time the phone rings."

"What happened with Martha?" I ask. "With Rita, I mean?"

"That same day, with Sadie's blood all over her, she came to the club looking for me. Fortunately, we overpowered her. Me and some of the men. Some of them are sitting over there at the bar right now, as it happens. No one died, but there were injuries. To the men, to her."

William leans back on the couch, and it looks like he's

wincing at some hidden pain. "She was like a wild dog. There's a devil in that woman, Angie."

He reaches into his side pocket and pulls out a wallet. Rummages through the sleeves, takes out an old photograph and hands it to me.

"Look at that."

"What is it?"

"That's Rita when she was twenty-three."

I take the photo. So weird to actually hold a photo in this day and age. The colour is faded and dull. But it's clear enough. It's Martha – Rita – and she's stunning. A firecracker. She's standing on a scenic rural road with a cluster of snow-topped mountains in the background, wearing the Road Wolves patch like it was made for her. The classic biker chick. Her tight denims hug a curvy figure, and there's a defiant expression on her face as she looks at the camera, a beer bottle in one hand and a cigarette dangling off her ruby red lips.

"Holy shit."

"Changed a bit, hasn't she?"

"Just a bit."

I hand the photo back to William. Maybe it's the beer, maybe it's William's stories, but I'm starting to feel a bit lightheaded.

"What happened after she cut up Sadie?"

William slips the photo back into his wallet. "The club ordered her to stay away from me and Tommy while we sorted out the divorce."

"Tommy. That's your son?"

"Aye. And I was more than okay with getting rid of her. But ... Rita and rejection. You know how that song goes, eh?"

William labours his way off the couch, walking stiffly

over to the pool table. It's like watching a once mighty silverback shrinking before my eyes. His haggard face shies from the dim lightbulb on the ceiling.

"She kept breaking the rules. Kept coming to the house at all times of day and night, and it would inevitably get ugly. Tommy was terrified of her. Quite frankly, so was I. The club didn't want to take it too far, but Rita left us with no choice."

"What does that mean?"

"She was banished. Excommunicated from the club. But that's not what broke her."

"No?"

"She became obsessed with seeing Tommy. Right up until the day Tommy told her never to come back. It was the *way* he told her. You knew he meant it. Even Rita, in her madness, could see it. It killed something inside her."

William shrugs, knuckles his tired eyes.

"Long story short. She disappeared, and at some point over the years, Rita Morrison became this other person. Rita Hunter. Martha Hunter. It's Martha Hunt now."

"When did you find out about that?"

"About what?"

"About the change of identity."

He nods. "Years later. That was a shock, I can tell you. She'd been busy with fake IDs, fake paperwork, fake passports. And recently, within the last six months, she's been showing up at Tommy's front door, trying to get back into his life. There's a grandchild now, you see, and Rita thinks she's got a right to be involved in the child's upbringing. That's what we were arguing about yesterday at the bus stop. I'm acting on behalf of Tommy and his wife, telling her to stay away."

"She didn't look too happy about it," I say.

"Well, I think that's enough talking for one night." He gives me a weary smile. "I don't think I've strung so many words together for years."

"Thank you, William," I say simply.

"One last thing, Angie."

William gives me the hard stare again. He takes out his phone, navigating his thumb over the screen. He flips it around. Shows me a photo of an older woman standing in a dimly lit kitchen, unable or unwilling to meet the camera's gaze. Her face is a map of scars. Life-changing scars that destroyed a pretty face. I can only imagine the sort of vicious, violent hatred that produced those wounds.

"Sadie?"

William nods. "Be wary of her, Angie. Be very wary. She's in a foul mood because of Tommy, and if you ask me, it sounds like she's taking it out on you."

I hand back the phone.

William takes it, then lowers his voice. "Call the police. You won't hear me saying that often, but in your case, I'll make an exception. Call the police, Angie. Do *not* tackle her by yourself."

"I was hoping not to get the police involved," I repeat, a little pathetically.

"Get them involved," he growls. "This is hard enough for an old outlaw like me to say, but you play this one by the book, okay? Get a restraining order. Do it, Angie. That might be enough to scare her off."

He walks over to the door but stops with his fingers on the handle. He stares back at me. Once again, it feels like I'm looking at a fading giant.

"She's a monster," he says. "Don't ever forget that."

CHAPTER EIGHTEEN

I'm standing beside Mum's grave when I make my decision. A decision that I hope will get Martha out of my life forever.

It's just after ten in the morning. The sky is a sheet of bleak grey, lingering low above the cemetery. A gentle drizzle has been falling all morning.

Last night, after getting home from the Road Wolves clubhouse, I found myself thinking a lot about Mum. I don't know what took me away from Martha and back to Mum. Just driving home, certain things seemed so much clearer as if I was objectively viewing my life from afar. How I've always run from what happened to her. To me. How I felt this overriding sense of shame about what Mum left me with, instead of pitying her for what she went through.

I went to bed feeling like a coward. Which makes it all the stranger that I slept like a baby and woke up with an unfamiliar lightness, as if a heavy burden had been removed while I slept. I felt so bold in fact that, after breakfast and a hot shower, I decided to do something I hadn't done in a long time. Visit Mum's grave.

I made the thirty-minute drive to the cemetery. Did a lot of thinking on the way. There were two possible options in front of me when it came to dealing with Martha. Call the police, as Dan, William and Claire had suggested, or visit her caravan again for a direct confrontation. The horror story that William had told me about Sadie didn't make me feel too comfortable about the latter option. But I still wasn't comfortable with calling the police. What if they dismissed me? What if they made me feel like I was wasting their time again? Maybe Claire would back me up? What about William? I doubted William would talk to the police.

After parking up, I walked through the entrance, still able to remember the way to Mum's grave despite how long it's been since I was last here. The cemetery is massive. Hilly and well kept. The original wooded section of the cemetery behind the watch-tower gateway has several graves dating back to the early eighteenth century. As I followed the path, I listened to the trees swaying in the wind.

I took a left turn and walked through a section of more modern graves. Another left turn. Down a narrow path that's flanked by older headstones than the ones near the cemetery gate. She's down there, middle of the row and somewhere on the right.

I could see it before I was even close. That's when I stopped. And for about a minute, I couldn't take my eyes off it.

Mum's grave, covered in spray paint.

I STARE AT THE DAMAGE. It's everywhere, front and back. On the top, around the edges. The message is clear too, unlike the random explosion of spray paint that she decorated my car with.

BURN BITCH!

Same words on the back.

At first, something snaps in my head. I actually hear it go like there's a piece of elastic in my skull that's been pulled to breaking point. At that moment, I have no intention of reasoning with Martha or calling the police. I'll go to her caravan and break her face.

It's not just paint. There's a large pile of faecal matter in front of Mum's grave, which I assume is dog mess that Martha has bagged from somewhere nearby. Looks like it came from a dog the size of a horse.

There is another and much more disgusting alternative. I try to push that assumption out of my thoughts.

How did she even find Mum's grave in the first place? I guess there are online references to what happened and perhaps newspaper clippings that mention the funeral and the aftermath. After all, I found Martha's caravan thanks to the internet.

I wonder how long she spent walking back and forth, searching for Mum? With all those cans of spray paint in her bag. With a bag of dog shit she'd picked up for the occasion.

I can't even cry. I'm too numb. Too angry.

It's always been a modest but tidy headstone. Mum's boss, Mr Wren, whom she worked for at the bakery, made sure that Mum was buried respectfully, and I remember that he even gave up his own plot in the cemetery to make sure it happened. He liked her. He might even have loved her. A shy man, I recall. Not the sort to speak his feelings. Well, this was one way to show his affection for her. He wanted to make sure that she had a gravestone and that she wasn't lost forever in an anonymous grave or cremated and scattered somewhere without meaning. It was nice of him, decent. I was too young to thank him properly at the time.

I've avoided this place. *That* was the coward in me. That's what I'm really angry about.

William is right. She's a monster.

Nothing but nothing justifies this.

I pull out my phone, standing under the gentle rain. I call Dan and tell him what's happened. He's about to go nuts on the other end when I cut him off.

"I'm ready to go to the police," I tell him.

"What's that?" Dan asks.

There's no hesitation in my voice.

"I need to get a restraining order on Martha."

CHAPTER NINETEEN

It works.

Dan and I talk to the police. From there we get a solicitor and make an application to the court for a Non-Harassment Order, also known as an Interdict. I have to outline all the specific incidents of harassment since Martha first entered our lives, which is not an easy process for me.

The court considers the order, and it's granted.

I can only imagine the look on Martha's face when the order is served at her caravan door. Despite being terrified of her, there's a part of me that wishes I could've been there to see it. It's the least I deserve after all she's put me through.

In the end, I needn't have worried about the police. The people I dealt with were supportive from the beginning, as was our Edinburgh-based solicitor. I had a lot of help and support, most of all from Dan, who's been my rock.

That's it. That's how I'm finally able to move on with my life and put this nightmare behind me. I've still got a lot of things to work on, but that's alright. I'm doing better because the days and weeks are ticking by and there's no more

Martha. Those first few days after the restraining order was issued were hard to say the least, and even now I keep thinking she'll show up sooner or later.

The floorboards still creak in the house, sometimes without a noticeable gust of wind to trigger them. I still check the locks every hour. I'm nervous when I park my car on deliveries, and I'm never quite sure what I'm going to come back to.

I have to pinch myself when a full day goes by and nothing has happened. Then I remind myself that she left Claire alone. It *is* possible. Maybe Martha found someone else to torment (I hope not), or she's so caught up in trying to see her grandchild that she doesn't have time for me anymore.

Very slowly, I'm accepting the inevitable conclusion.

It's over.

The nightmare is over.

PART 2

GLENCOE

CHAPTER TWENTY

The speedboat cuts through the glassy water of Loch Leven.

"Faster!" Dan yells. "Faster, faster!"

There's a light whooshing sensation in the pit of my stomach, and it feels like my feet are lifting off the ground.

"Faster," Dan repeats, cupping his hands over his mouth so he can make himself heard above the engine. "C'mon, Mike. We can go faster than this."

I nudge him on the arm with my elbow. It's quite a sharp dig, and I'm lucky it doesn't land on his ribs by mistake.

"This is fast enough."

Michael Laing, standing at the wheel of the boat, turns his head back and salutes Dan to let him know the message is received and understood. He's got one of those well-trimmed beards that looks like it's been pencilled on. To me, he looks too boyish for a man in his early forties. Soft, tanned skin. Not a wrinkle in sight.

At Dan's request, he speeds up the boat. It's another opportunity to show off to his supermodel girlfriend, Darcie, who hails from Berlin. She stands beside him at the wheel, clapping and squealing with excitement. A tall, bronzed goddess who still looks amazing wrapped up in a warm jacket over a fleece pullover. And not the brainless bimbo I'd expected (or secretly hoped) she'd be. Turns out she's a doctor.

For the past hour, we've been doing high-speed loops in a secluded part of Loch Leven, close to the Laing house, where we have the water all to ourselves.

An explosion of spray shoots up from behind the boat. There's an excited yelp from Liza, who is Jonny Laing's twenty-seven-year-old girlfriend. Half American, half Ecuadorian. A fledgling actress who divides her time between apartments in London, Los Angeles and New York. Not bad for a "fledgling".

"Faster!" Liza yells, echoing Dan. "Faster!"

The boat speeds its way across the loch to the sound of whooping and laughter. Meanwhile, the sun dips behind the shadowy mountains of Glencoe. I have to admit, it's spectacular. It feels like I'm living in a painting. The sky is clear, and the rugged scenery and its furnishings glow with seasonal colourings, the deep reds, yellows and oranges.

It's been a good day, I think as Michael finally steers the boat towards the shallows. I hold on to Dan's arm, then loosen my grip as the boat approaches the private jetty. I've never been much of a "water" person, and it's always a relief to feel solid ground under my feet.

Sure, it's been a good day, but I'm tired now. The Laings and their girlfriends are nice people, but they're like puppies who don't ever nap. Always switched on, always wanting to do something. Nonetheless, this introvert is grateful to be here. Looking around at the mountainous scenery, how could anyone be anything but grateful to be here?

The weather gods have smiled on us since Dan and I arrived in Glencoe, almost one year on from our failed road trip when we decided to turn back. Surrounded by Munros, it's not hard to see why Loch Leven is rated as one of the most scenic lochs in Scotland. Once the V-shaped disturbance of the speedboat recedes, the water becomes still again, and in the fading daylight, it's nothing short of majestic. It's like watching the loch go back to sleep. Sure, it's cold, but I've always been a sucker for autumn.

Nonetheless, it's that time of year again.

Mum's anniversary.

This November it'll be thirty-three years since the fire. Dan and I are still committed to going on holiday at this time of year, so here we are. Just like last year, we started with a short road trip on the A82, spending a couple of nights en route, soaking up the glorious scenery and travelling north at a (very) leisurely pace. As for the pets, my friend Meghan is staying at our house, looking after Billie Jean and Brogan. We've been getting photos and updates on a daily basis, and I do trust these photos. Also, they aren't just close-ups. And also, I'm not getting them every single hour of the day.

We can relax. The pets and the house are in good hands.

We can enjoy this. We *deserve* to enjoy this.

The build-up to Mum's anniversary this year has been different. It feels like I'm making progress, and I suspect it has something to do with the Martha situation last year. Getting through that nightmare. Going to the police, getting the Non-Harassment Order. It would've been easier to run away from Martha like I ran away from what happened to Mum for years. Run away, hope that she'd get bored and leave me alone. But I did something. I found Claire, questioned William, took out the restraining order. I haven't heard from Martha in a year. Not a peep. I guess sometimes it pays to face down the danger instead of running away and hiding. This realisation was more empowering than all the therapy sessions combined.

Apart from that, life is the same. I'm still a struggling writer who delivers food at night. But things are happening. The book is taking shape, and I've jotted down a solid list of small publishers who might be interested in taking it on.

I visited Mum's grave before we left for Glencoe. The spray paint has long since been removed and the headstone refreshed with a new inscription that begins ... *Beloved mother.*

THE SIX OF us walk back to the house along the edge of the loch. Spirits are high after the boat trip, and it's hard not to get caught up in the overall, infectious sense of enthusiasm that permeates the group. It'll catch up with me later in terms of draining my introvert body battery. It always does.

"Are we going to the pub, then?" Jonny asks in his hybrid accent. Sometimes he jumps from one end of Britain to another within a single sentence. Definitely sounds like a Scotsman who's spent too much time in London. Jonny is suntanned and possesses the same smooth, boyish features as his younger brother. When they walk side by side, I can't help but think of a pair of Ken dolls.

"Sounds good," Michael says. "Darcie, pub?"

She smiles and wraps her long, skinny arm around his waist.

"I'm in, Mikey."

I smile. She calls him *Mikey* like he's a little boy. She's much taller than he is and has to lean over to give him a peck on the cheek. Darcie and Liza then break off from the pack and walk beside the water, arm in arm.

"What about you guys?" Jonny asks, looking at Dan and me.

Dan puts an arm around my shoulder. "Oh, I don't know. What do you think, Angie? Hungry?"

What else am I going to say?

"I could eat."

This is pretty much what the holiday has looked like so far. Late starts and long brunches followed by activities and then a trip to the pub, which is inside the local hotel, also nestled on the banks of the loch.

The best part of the trip is the amount of writing I'm getting done. In contrast to this time last year, the words are pouring out of me. Good words. Meaningful words that take the story somewhere. I'm caught up in the manuscript to the point of obsession, and I don't remember it feeling like this for a long time. Truth be told, I'd happily skip the speedboat rides and pub visits to sit in front of the laptop and work on my novel. Unlike Dan, I'm not much of a socialiser, and the more time I spend around the Laings, the more exhausted I become. I crave a little solitude here and there, but I have to remember my manners and why I'm here in the first place. I'm only enjoying the fruits of this environment because I'm their guest.

Still, I work every chance I get.

THE NIGHTS up here are the quietest I've ever known.

I can't get used to it. It's so different from the quiet in

cities and towns, where there's always something humming away in the background. The sound of distant traffic. Voices in the street. In our case, a creaky old house that groans every time the wind blows.

This is different. And with such absolute silence, I can't help but fill it with thoughts of Mum, life, the universe – and the meaning of it all. Thoughts I've always had, but they've never seemed so loud. It's like someone else in the bedroom talking to me, and sometimes it feels like my inner voice is loud enough to wake up Dan as he sleeps beside me.

I switch positions on the bed. Lie on my side, my back. Turn the pillow over. I can't decide if I'm hot or cold.

Dan turns onto his back and starts snoring. It's gentle enough at first, rapidly progressing to the ridiculous. How can he sleep so effortlessly? I should be tired, too, after everything we've done today (and after three glasses of white wine at the pub), but I'm wide awake, staring up at the ceiling. The guest rooms in the Laing house are quaint and spacious. Tartan carpets, solid oak furniture and, to my delight, a writing desk that offers a stunning view of the loch. There's an en suite bathroom, and if they had a fridge, I could happily stay in this room for the entire trip and work on my book.

Dan would love that.

Maybe it's the story buzzing around my head, keeping me awake. If I had the room to myself or if I were at home, I'd be writing.

The hoot of an owl shatters the silence. I lift my head off the pillow and see a glimmer of moonlight sneaking past the curtains. My head's still up when I hear something else from outside. Something that definitely isn't an owl.

I sit up in bed, my heart thumping.

Did I imagine that? There's a digital clock beside the bed, and I glance at it.

1:43 a.m.

"Dan?"

Then I hear it again. Footsteps. There's no mistaking what I'm hearing – that's the sound of someone walking outside the house. Sounds like they're right at the back door.

I whisper louder. "Dan?"

He doesn't stir, and if anything, his cartoonish snoring gets louder. I push back the sheets and creep across the bedroom on my tiptoes.

C'mon, I tell myself. *It's nothing.*

I stop by the large window. Peel back the curtains a few inches, opening up a small gap that'll let me look outside. A column of moonlight, grey with a bluish tinge, spills through the gap. Our bedroom looks out towards the back of the Laing house. A beautiful view by day. At night, acres of darkness. There's an old cottage somewhere down there. I've seen it from afar and assume that it was used by live-in staff back in the day. Apart from the cottage, there's not a lot to see except for empty fields that stretch down to the unspoiled forests in the distance.

Crunch-crunch-crunch.

There's someone walking around in the garden.

"What the hell?" I whisper.

I peek outside again. Whoever's out there, they're so close to the building that I won't be able to take a good look at them unless I open the window and poke my head outside.

I turn the latch on the window while light footsteps skip along the gravel. Playful. Childlike. My heart is in my mouth. I don't want to do this. I don't want to know. There's a split-second sensation of pure horror awakening inside me. Of old wounds reopening.

Someone is down there. Someone is trying to get into the Laing house and—

An outburst of giggling cuts off my train of thought.

A tall silhouette comes into view, racing from the back of the house and onto the grass. A beam of light shudders in the runner's hand. A torch? The silhouette keeps running, emerging onto a small island of moonlight close to the cottage. It's a woman. She's tall and, as the moonlight reveals, naked. Someone else comes into the light. A man who's been giving chase, and he's also naked in the moonlight.

Finally, they talk. I recognise the voices immediately.

It's Jonny and Liza.

They keep running and, eventually, disappear behind a cluster of trees and into darkness. Muffled screams. More giggles.

I jump back from the window before they see me. I stay put for a while, trying to get my heart to slow down. What are they doing running around in their birthday suits in the freezing cold? Forget it. I don't want to know. Fucking rich people, they're wired differently.

I hope Dan doesn't wake up right now. Fortunately, he's still snoring his head off, and after another minute of deep breathing, I tiptoe my way back into bed. Then it's back to staring at the ceiling again. Back to a horrible churning sensation in the pit of my stomach. I don't get it. There's nothing to worry about, and still this underlying anxiety threatens to bubble up back to the surface.

It's only Jonny and Liza, I tell myself.

After that, I lie awake for hours, listening to the silence. Waiting for a noise outside that doesn't come.

CHAPTER TWENTY-ONE

I walk back to the house after a good day of writing in the hotel pub. I've got that warm, fuzzy feeling in my bones. I feel both light and full. It feels like I'm doing what I was meant to do, and when I'm in a flow state like this, life doesn't feel like swimming upstream twenty-four hours a day. Count me in.

And no matter what happens with the book, whether it flops or kickstarts my career as an author, all the hours of toiling away will have been worth it.

Because I'll have made something.

I just want it to sell, that's all. Creative, critical and commercial glory. That's not too much to ask, is it?

We've been so lucky with the weather since coming to Glencoe, and today is another winner. The short walk back to the Laing house from the hotel is so pleasant that I decide to prolong it by sitting down at the edge of the loch.

I cross my legs and stare out at the calm water.

Today, I managed to dodge a road trip with the Laings and their girlfriends. After a sleepless night, I told Dan I couldn't handle all that extrovert energy. It's only Dan's opinion that really matters to me. He knows how important my work is and that I don't need to be on a speedboat or rock climbing every other afternoon to be entertained. We had a brief conversation in the bedroom about it before going downstairs for breakfast. He was fine with it, reminding me that it's my holiday too and that he only wants me to be happy.

At the breakfast table, I mentioned a headache to the others, possibly a mild hangover and the need for a lie-down. The Laings, as well as Liza and Darcie, have no idea that I'm working on my book during this trip. When they ask what I did later, I'll tell them I took a stroll around the loch and sat on the bank, reading and putting my feet up. They won't care if I withdraw a little. I wouldn't if it were the other way around.

So while the others went on a road trip with the intention of hiking to the Lost Valley in Glencoe, I took a short walk to the hotel. Found a nice seat with a view of the loch. Laptop open and it was bliss. A good – no, *great* writing session – fuelled by coffee and sandwiches and the best lemon sponge cake I've ever tasted. I was in there all day, and it was quite possibly the best writing session of my life. To say I'm on a high as I walk back to the Laing house would be a major understatement.

I sit by the water for an hour, thinking about Mum's anniversary. Tomorrow is November fifteenth. It's come around again, but I won't go to pieces. I feel pretty certain about that.

Last night *was* a bit weird. There was a moment where I did go wobbly at the knees, but I guess it's understandable. I'm in a strange house in the country, and it's a far cry from what I'm used to back at home. I have no idea why Jonny and Liza were running around naked at daft o'clock in the morning. Again, rich people. And considering everything that happened last year, it's no surprise I was a bit jumpy. Doesn't mean that November fifteenth is winning. Far from it.

It's with some reluctance that I get up and walk back to the house. Jonny's car is still gone when I get there, which means the others haven't come back yet.

Nice, I think, trudging up the long driveway. My back is a little stiff from sitting all day, but it was worth it.

I drop my rucksack at the door, and instead of going straight into the house, I wander around the back for a look at the old cottage. It was Darcie who told me that the cottage had been there long before the Laing house was even built. I don't think anyone knows how old it is. Once the Laing house went up in the mid-eighties, the cottage became something of a footnote. Now it's rotting in the shadow of the mansion, not having been modernised in any way.

I walk over the gravel, veering onto a well-worn path that starts at the edge of the grass. It's dry. The ground makes a delightful crunch under my shoes as I walk. A flat surface turns into a slight downhill that offers a stunning view of green fields and distant woodland. Michael told me that red deer stags sometimes come out of the woods and make their way up to the mansion. Jonny says he's seen golden eagles flying over the house too. I have no idea whether I believe them or not.

It's the cottage that holds my attention. I stop in front and take a good look. I'm no renovation expert, but I'm pretty sure this could be an attractive building if someone went to the bother of restoring it. Maybe an Airbnb or something like that? There's no shortage of funds, but the Laings don't have live-in staff anymore, and there are enough guest rooms in the mansion to leave the cottage as a worn-out relic that's outlived its usefulness. As for an Airbnb, they probably don't want strangers hanging around. I get that.

Looking at the cottage now, I'd guess it's at least a hundred years old and maybe even two hundred. Single-storey building, two windows on either side of a weathered wooden door that's peeling paint from top to bottom. The metal hardware around the door is caked in rust. It's not a building that screams hello.

I look towards the house. I should go back and wait for the others to return. And yet something pulls me forward. I try the handle. It feels jagged and flimsy.

"Hello?" I say.

What am I doing? No one's lived here for decades.

My shoulder nudges the door, and it creaks open.

A powerful odour hits my nostrils as I take a tentative step inside. Whatever it is, it's musty and overpowering. By just opening the door, it feels like I've released something vile that's been trapped in there for decades. I cough into the back of my hand and think about backing off. About going back to the big house. A cup of tea would be nice.

I walk further into the cottage.

It's gloomy, but there's enough light coming through the windows for me to see well enough. Still, I flick the old light switch even though I know there's a snowball's chance in hell of a light coming on. No great loss. There's not much to look at. I see some ancient pieces of furniture lying around – a couple of wooden chairs and a flaccid old couch that's ripped open at the sides and across the armrests. Looks like it's been set upon by a pack of wild dogs. The dusty remains of a bulky Panasonic TV sits in the corner. Tall bookshelves, covered in dust, are sparsely decorated with faded paperbacks.

I'm reluctant to walk too far from the door. There's this irrational fear of being locked in that I can't shake. Of walking in further and hearing the door slam shut behind me. Then the turn of the key in the lock and a cruel laugh.

Got you.

Enough. I force myself to walk further in, and to do that I step over the remains of a dead mouse. *Sorry*, I think, not sure what I'm sorry for. I browse the living room, whistling on autopilot to calm myself down. Sometimes I hum for the same reason. Allowing myself to speed up a little, I walk down the narrow hallway and turn the corner into a dusty and rancid-smelling kitchen. That's stale urine in the air, I'm sure of it.

The counter is bare except for dust and hundreds of dead flies.

My stomach clenches tight.

There's a cup sitting on the counter, and among everything else in the cottage, it sticks out like a sore thumb. It looks brand new. No dust. There's a picture of Mickey Mouse on the side, grinning, both thumbs sticking up. The images isn't faded. It's crystal clear.

I move towards the counter for a closer look. Leaning over, I look inside the cup and see a small puddle of brownish liquid at the bottom. Leftover cold tea? How is that possible?

"Shit," I say.

My veins fill with icy terror. Time stops in the little cottage, and everything else besides the shiny Mickey Mouse cup blurs into the background. Before I know it, I'm backing out of the kitchen, retracing my steps down the hallway. I sprint out the front door as if there's a leopard chasing me.

My lungs gasp for air.

The relief I feel at being outside is overwhelming. But I don't hang around. It's getting dark, and those distant woods have already begun to fade into the gloom.

I walk fast. And when I'm halfway back to the house, my walk turns into a run.

CHAPTER TWENTY-TWO

It's November fifteenth.

I wake up early and without an alarm. We forgot to pull the curtains last night, and it's so bright and sunny outside that yesterday's strange visit to the cottage is fading like a bad dream.

There was a cup in the kitchen. So what? A cup that, to my eye at least, looked like it had been used recently. There are plenty of explanations that I didn't bother to consider before I rushed out of the cottage like a total idiot.

I got spooked. No big deal.

Dan brings me breakfast in bed like it's my birthday. It's a bit obvious, but he means well. Looks like we're doing happy faces, judging by the mega-grin on his face as he carries the tray into the bedroom. He holds it aloft, mimicking a waiter in a fancy restaurant. I'm not much of a breakfast person (or a morning person for that matter), but he gets it right with a plate of toast, coffee, orange juice and a blueberry muffin.

He sits on the edge of the bed while I eat. Neither one of us has said the words "November fifteenth" yet, and I think that's the way we're going to play it. It's just an ordinary day. Angie will *not* lose her shit.

"I've got some grapes downstairs in the fridge if you want them?" Dan says. "Red and seedless. Only the finest."

"This'll do for now," I say. I haven't made much of a dent in the food he's brought. "But thanks."

His eyes linger on me.

"What is it, Dan?"

"There's been some talk," he says.

"About what?"

"About plans for tonight."

"Oh."

I feel a pinch of relief. For a second, I thought Dan was going to bring up my impromptu visit to the cottage yesterday. Maybe someone saw me go in there. Saw me sprinting out, my face as white as a sheet. Saw me running back to the big house. Wouldn't necessarily be a bad thing if they did bring it up. I could ask someone about that cup. That *new* cup in a ramshackle building full of old things.

"Jonny and Michael are talking about this club night," Dan says. "It's happening over at the hotel."

I take a sip of coffee, and it's good. Really good. The Laings have a fantastic espresso machine in the kitchen. One that costs well over a grand.

"Club night?"

Dan gives me a playful tap on the shoulder. "Yeah, club night! They're putting on a nineties-themed party in the basement. Fancy dress. The DJ is going to be playing all the greatest hits of the day – Nirvana, Oasis, Blur, you know? Mike says it's an annual thing."

"Sounds fun."

He nods. "Yeah. I was non-committal downstairs when they brought it up. Didn't know how you'd feel about it."

"Hmm."

"So ... you wanna go?"

I stare down into the black pool of coffee, and while Dan sits on the bed waiting for an answer, my thoughts are pulled back to the cottage. There was tea in that cup. A small puddle of cold tea. Who left it there? Was it one of the Laings? Darcie? Liza? I haven't seen any one of them show the slightest bit of interest in the cottage.

The bright sunlight calls me back.

Fuck, I think. I'm acting weird, and guess what, campers? It's that time of year again. Can't be a coincidence, can it? Then again, it was never going to be that easy just to sail through one more dreaded November fifteenth. It'll be better, though. *I'll* be better.

"Angie?"

Dan's voice sounds like it's coming from the other side of the house. But he's still on the bed, still right in front of me.

"What?"

"Wakey-wakey. I thought you'd fallen asleep with your eyes open."

"Sorry. What did you say?"

"We were talking about the nineties night at the hotel," Dan says, shifting closer on the bed. "Listen, we don't have to dress up. I'm sure Jonny and Michael will go as the Gallagher brothers or whatever, but we can just say we didn't bring anything suitable. We could just go for a couple of hours and—"

He stops. Gives me a knowing nod.

"You don't want to go, do you?"

Maybe someone was doing some work around the house yesterday. Or in the garden while I was at the hotel. And they went inside the cottage to take a break, to get out of the sun, and forgot about the Mickey Mouse cup they left there.

"Angie?"

"What's that?"

"You don't want to go, do you?"

I shake my head. "Sorry. I hate to be a spoilsport."

Dan leans in closer. Starts rubbing his thumb on my forearm like I'm a child who's woken up from a nightmare. "Hey, it's fine. There's no pressure. The last thing I want to do is pressure you."

I put the coffee down on the tray and reach for his hand. He takes mine and gives it a gentle squeeze.

"I'd like to go," I say. "It's just … just I don't know if I'm ready to go out clubbing on the anniversary, you know? Not yet."

"Sure."

"I'm fully on board for what we're doing here. Turning the day around, making it a positive thing. That's why we're here. Clubbing? I'm not quite there."

"You're right," Dan says. "We'll take it slow."

"There's some good news, though," I say.

"Oh?"

"I have zero cravings for a therapy session. One step at a time, right?"

"Definitely," Dan says. "And hey, forget about the nineties night. Let the others dress up as Liam Gallagher or Kurt Cobain or whatever. We'll do our own thing, okay? Or we'll do nothing if that's what you'd prefer. Just say the word. Your wish is my command."

"My wish is your command?"

"Command me," he says, throwing in a mock bow.

"Okay then. I command you to go to the club night and have a good time with the others."

Dan sits up like he's been hit by an electrical shock. "No way. I'm not leaving you alone tonight."

"I'll be fine."

"Nope. No way."

I let go of his hand. "C'mon, Dan, it's the nineties. That's your favourite musical era. I'm not going to let you miss out on a good night just because I don't feel like it. You don't get to hang around with Jonny and Mike much. You should go."

He's shaking his head again. Hand up, like he's not going to entertain a discussion. "I'm not going."

"You're going," I tell him in a firm voice. "You just said my wish is your command."

"Angie—"

"Dan," I say, cutting him off, "listen, don't take this the wrong way, but I think I'd like to be alone tonight."

There's a look on his face like I just slapped him.

"Alone?"

"Yeah."

"Why?"

All I can manage is a feeble one-shouldered shrug. Then I turn my attention back to the tray. Scrape the second piece of toast off the plate and take a bite. I chew, but I'm struggling to find my appetite and, at the same time, get my mind off that Mickey Mouse cup. "Not sure. But I am sure I won't be good company."

"Like I care about that."

"Well, I do."

"I know, Angie," he says with a sudden grin. "I know why you want to be on your own tonight."

"Do tell, Sherlock."

"You want to zone out and do some writing. You want the rest of us out of the way."

I smile. "Maybe."

His face relaxes a little. "Okay. Guess I won't be complaining when Netflix turn this masterpiece of yours into a hit movie."

"Yeah, and that's the only way *you'll* read it. Through a TV screen."

Dan laughs and then goes quiet for a minute. Finally, he gives a curt nod of the head. "Okay. I'll go for a couple of hours. But I'm coming back early, so you get your writing done, and then we can hang out here together."

"Thanks," I say. "You're a star."

At my insistence, he goes back downstairs to join the others in the kitchen. I want to tell him about the cup, but I don't want to worry him. Not today of all days. What would he think if I started banging on about finding a Mickey Mouse cup in the cottage? It sounds like nothing. It probably *is* nothing. But still, I know Dan. He'd never leave my side.

Something else Dan doesn't know is that I've got no desire to work. This is the first day of the holiday that I haven't felt the itch. November fifteenth – what a coincidence.

It's fine, I tell myself.

My phone pings on the bed. It's Meghan. She's sent us a fresh batch of photos of Billie Jean and Brogan, taken in the back garden yesterday and today. They look happy. They look healthy. I browse the images for a while, missing them both like crazy. Then I lie back on the bed, staring at the ceiling. Memorising every little detail.

Anything to ignore the sensation of that knot tightening in my stomach.

I TAKE A SHOWER, get dressed and go downstairs.

The others have long since finished breakfast and are in the living room now. I'm the last one there, making it six out of six. Michael wastes no time in trying to tempt me into going to the club night at the hotel.

"It'll be amazing," he says, taking up a position in the middle of the living room. He's still wearing his teal-coloured dressing gown, and he's got a pair of Adidas trainers on his feet. "These things can be a bit cheesy, but they're a lot of fun."

I nod. "I'm sure it will be."

"Not only fun," Michael says. "They're packed. *Rammed*. All the yokels descend from their huts in the hills, and it's another excuse for them to go mad."

Jonny chimes in from the massive L-shaped sofa. He's watching something on his iPad, which rests on his lap. "He's right. You don't want to miss tonight, Angie. It'll be nothing if not entertaining."

"Remember what we spoke about, guys," Dan says, walking into the living room with a glass of fresh orange juice. He hands it to me with a subtle wink. "It's a delicate time of year."

"Huh?" Michael says.

"Delicate," Dan repeats. And then he lowers his voice. "Remember, remember the fifteenth of November?"

I can almost hear the machinery squeaking in the Laings' heads. In the end, it's Jonny who reboots first.

"Ohhhh, right. Yeah."

"Forgot about that," Michael says, copping on or at least pretending to. "Gotcha now. Yeah, cool. Sorry, eh?"

"Next time," I say. "I'll definitely be there."

"Cool," Jonny says. His eyes widen as if a lightbulb just switched on above his head. Then to Dan and his brother, "Well, there is another solution if Angie doesn't want to come to the hotel with us."

I don't like where this is going.

Jonny continues, "The five of us go to the club night for a few hours, find the most interesting people and bring the party back here. Sound like a plan?"

Michael nods. "Yeah. Bring the party back to casa del Laing. We can break out the champagne and—"

"No," I say quickly. "Don't do that."

The Laing brothers look at me.

"No?" Jonny asks.

"I want you guys to have a great time," I say. "And that means staying to the end. To the *very* end. How late does this nineties-themed night go?"

Michael scratches his pencilled-on beard. "About three, I think."

"Stay till then."

That's how we leave it. The activity schedule for the rest of the morning and afternoon is left open for people to do whatever they want. The three couples will go their separate ways, and the plan is to meet up later in the day. After Darcie and Liza come back from their walk by the loch, Jonny and Liza head off for a drive (with their clothes on, I hope), and Michael and Darcie take a ride on the speedboat.

Dan and I are still in the house long after the others have gone. Catching our breath, that's about as far as our plans go.

We're far more boring and prone to stillness than the Laings. And that's fine with me. Dan's scrolling through his phone, and I'm stretched out on the L-shaped couch, resting my eyes. I still don't want to work, and I don't expect the writing mojo to make much of an appearance today. Maybe later. So far, I'm doing good. Getting through November fifteenth without losing my shit.

I open my eyes. Glance across the room.

"Dan?"

He looks up from his phone. "Hmm?"

"Can I ask you something?"

"Go ahead."

"What's the deal with that cottage at the back of the house?"

"The cottage? Don't know much about it. That it was there for decades, long before the Laings showed up – I know that much. I think a housekeeper used to live there in the eighties and nineties. Mrs ... Och, I don't know. She died years ago."

"And it's been empty ever since?"

"Think so. Why?"

"I had a look inside the other day."

That doesn't seem to faze him. "And?"

"It's what you'd expect for the most part. Old and run-down. Dead mouse on the floor, and it stinks of piss."

I sit up on the couch. My face feels flushed, and I wonder if the heating in the house is turned up too high. I take off my hoodie and let my arms breathe.

"Except ..."

Dan's looking at his phone again. "Except what?"

I hesitate, not knowing if what I'm about to say will give Dan cause to worry. I don't want that. Not today of all days.

"There was a cup on the kitchen counter," I tell him. "This Mickey Mouse cup that just ... just looked out of place."

"Out of place how?"

"Well, it was this brand-new thing in the cottage. One new thing while everything else was old and falling apart. But get this. There was tea in it. Like somebody had left it sitting there that morning. The Laings don't have live-in staff anymore, do they?"

Dan's still looking at his phone, which means I haven't totally freaked him out yet. "Not live-in. But there's an old guy, Albert, who cuts the grass, and I think they've got a cleaning company that visits once a week."

"Would they have any reason to go into the cottage?"

"How would I know?"

"Right. Sorry."

The conversation fizzles out, and Dan goes back to mindless scrolling on the internet. I still have that insect-crawling-up-the-back-of-my-neck feeling, and it doesn't stop when I tell myself that it's just a cup and that, yes, it's probably this Alfred or Albert guy or someone from the cleaning company who left it there.

It was ... *out of place.*

It's Mum's anniversary, which I know means I'm liable to obsess over the little things. Compared to previous years, overthinking the existence of a cup is harmless. If that's the worst thing that happens today, I'll be doing okay. I don't need to aspire to perfection. I'll settle for each year getting a little better.

"Don't suppose you've changed your mind about the club night?" Dan asks, looking up again. "Go on, you know you want to. Pretty sure you'll get some Alanis Morissette if you ask the DJ nicely."

I shake my head.

"No. And don't let Jonny or Michael bring the party back here. Please."

"They won't. They're all talk anyway. They'll be fast asleep in the corner by midnight while their young girlfriends are dancing the night away. Neither Michael nor Jonny are as young as they like to think they are."

"You could have fooled me," I say.

Dan laughs. He rubs his forefinger and thumb together. "I can't imagine what Liza and Darcie see in them, can you?"

"They're sweet," I say, feeling guilty that we're slagging off our hosts behind their backs. "It's nice of them to ask us up here."

"And you're okay?" Dan asks. "Besides obsessing about Mickey Mouse cups in creepy old cottages?"

I smile despite a gnawing discomfort chiselling at my insides. *Oh great. He's thinking about it now. Asking himself whether you're going nuts or not.*

"I'm fine."

"You sure?"

"Uh-huh."

Dan stands up, stretches his arms above his head and yawns. Then he comes over and sits down beside me on the stupidly expensive couch.

"We're doing okay, aren't we?"

"Yep."

He kisses me on the cheek, wraps an arm around me. I lean into him. He feels warm and safe like he always does. Still, my nostrils twitch at his aftershave.

"What's that?" I ask, gagging.

"It's one of Michael's."

"You'll be wanting a Ferrari next."

Dan's face lights up with mock excitement. "Michael has a Ferrari in London as a matter of fact. I was thinking about asking if he'd let me borrow it for a few months. You know? Just until my mid-life crisis subsides."

My elbow lands a playful dig in his ribs. It's a long time before either one of us says something after that.

"She'd want you to be happy," Dan says in a quiet voice. "You know that, don't you?"

"I've always known that."

"Good. You've survived this far, Ang. And I know I don't say it enough, but I'm proud of you."

I smile. "You are?"

Dan nods, holds my gaze. "And she would be too."

IT'S SEVEN O'CLOCK.

Dan, along with the Laings and their girlfriends, have just left to go to the hotel for "Nineties Madness!" That's the official title. They certainly look the part. The boys have kitted themselves out with Stone Roses bucket hats and baggy Adidas tracksuits and trainers. Meanwhile, Liza is rocking a Spice Girls Union Jack dress (where she sourced that from, I have no idea), and Darcie has nailed the Seattle grunge look with her faded flannel shirt and jeans. Even in tattered clothes and scruffy hair, she looks a million bucks. I have to ask where they got their outfits from, and it turns out they've been in the house all along. Nineties Madness, it seems, is a bit of a tradition. I wouldn't be surprised if it's the main reason Jonny and Michael come to Glencoe at this time of year.

The house is quiet. Too big for just one person, especially at night. I wish I had Brogan or Billie Jean with me. Just a little non-human company would be perfect to see out the rest of November fifteenth.

A steady rain falls outside. The wind is picking up, too, and some of the tree branches are slapping against the windows at the back of the house. It sounds like a giant knocking. Dan and the others decided against walking to the hotel and, with not much in the way of taxis or Ubers around here, drew straws to find a driver. Dan lost but, to his credit, remained in good spirits about being the taxi. I'm kind of relieved. He won't crawl into bed, stinking of drink. And his hands won't wander.

I stand in the kitchen, waiting for the kettle to boil. Listening to the rain.

In truth, it's the perfect weather for writing. So much so that I've decided to force myself to work even if it's the last thing I feel like doing. With any luck, I'll lose myself in the book once I get started. I abandon the tea. Pour myself a glass of white wine instead and bring the laptop into the living room. I sit cross-legged on the couch and measure the progress I've made so far on this trip. The novel is good. I can say that without sounding arrogant. All the pieces are coming together, but there's still plenty of work to do before I've got a solid draft.

I get comfortable. Open up the laptop and get to work. Except the words don't come. It's a case of total blockage, and I find myself staring at my old friend from last year, the blinking cursor. I browse my online music library, and that wastes a good five minutes. I select an ambient thriller soundtrack to help conjure up the right mood.

Nothing.

I get up, pace the room and pretend that I'm brainstorming. Sit down again, sip the wine and pour another when the glass is empty.

In the end, I give up and close the laptop. Scrolling through my phone, I find the happy photo of Mum. The one where she looks like a young Julie Christie. I stare at it and feel that longing for what might have been, an old wound that never heals.

Is this where I lose it like I've done every other year of my life? Maybe the wine wasn't such a good idea.

I get up again. Walk around the empty house with a glass of water to clear my head. Maybe I'll make that tea. Maybe I should've gone out with the others. Forced myself out of my comfort zone and passed the time in some other way than moping around a big, empty house. I feel like a ghost haunting myself.

I keep walking. I realise it feels just like making deliveries at night and being in the car. The constant movement is soothing.

I go upstairs. Wander back and forth for a while until I find myself back in our guest bedroom. With the light switched off, I drift towards the window as if drawn by the sound of the rain hitting the glass. I pull back the curtains. There'll be nothing out there, certainly no naked people.

A sea of darkness stretching out for miles. That's all.

Wait.

A wild, fluttering sensation in my stomach builds to such intensity that I feel like I'm about to throw up.

There is something.

I fall forward, press my hands and face against the glass. I push harder until my nose hurts.

I look outside, not wanting to believe my eyes. *It's the wine. It's exhaustion. It's November fifteenth.* But I keep looking until I'm certain that nothing is going to change. And nothing does.

It's real. This is really happening.

There's a light on.

There's a light on in the old cottage.

CHAPTER TWENTY-THREE

I hurry downstairs and grab my phone off the couch. Run back upstairs to the bedroom, and the first thing I do is check if the light is still on at the cottage. It's there. The living-room window. I watch it for a full minute before calling Dan. The call goes straight to voicemail.

"Shit."

My heart is back in my throat as I continue to watch the light. As I stand at the window, my mind scrambles for a rational explanation. Is it a light? Or is it just the reflection of the moonlight on the glass? That would make sense, wouldn't it? When I was in the cottage, I tried the living-room switch, and there was nothing. No bulb and I just assumed there wasn't any electricity running down there. But there isn't any moonlight either. The sky is clouded over tonight. What else? *Think of something.* Maybe someone went in there to clean earlier today, sorted the electricity and put in a fresh light bulb and left it switched on by mistake. Maybe? Maybe it's a two-day cleaning spree, and that's why there was a Mickey Mouse cup with tea still in the kitchen.

There shouldn't be anyone in there. Not at this time of night.

I try calling Dan again.

'Hi, this is Dan. Sorry I can't come to the phone right now, but if you leave your name and number, I'll call you back as soon as possible. Cheers.'

I'm about to leave a message, but something stops me. What will Dan think when he hears it? A freaked-out voicemail from Angie on November fifteenth. And that could be several hours from now, assuming that Nineties Madness is exciting enough to keep him distracted from his phone.

He'll think you're crazy.

Tonight of all nights.

I hang up.

There's only one thing left to do, and I can't run from that option anymore. Only one way to find out if I am crazy or dreaming or whether there really is someone in the cottage. I can stand here at the window all night, wishing the light away, but it's still burning. And it'll keep burning.

I have to go over there. I have to check it out.

I walk downstairs and head straight to the back door. After switching on the outdoor light, I step outside and feel the rain falling on my head. A blanket of clouds veils the stars. It feels like the darkest night yet.

There's a simple explanation for this, I tell myself. And I keep telling myself that, because the human capacity for delusion is remarkable. *It's just November fifteenth, that's all. Just November fifteenth.*

A voice screams in my head. It sounds like my aunt Rose.

Don't go out there.

I walk towards the cottage. My stride is robotic and

quick, as if by speeding up, I might be able to out walk the mounting sense of terror building up inside me.

I should call Dan again. If not Dan, then the police. Where is the nearest police station anyway?

No, I can't leave this any longer. It's up to me.

I step off the gravel and onto the wet grass. The ground doesn't crunch under my feet this time. It squelches. I glance over my shoulder. The Laing house, a gloomy gigantic silhouette, sinks into darkness, and as I turn back to face the cottage, I have the strangest feeling of being a character in a fairy tale, walking into a cursed forest.

The light pulls me closer. I have to be mindful of where I step. The back of the Laing house is only well groomed up to a point, and after that, it's a wilderness. That's deliberate, according to Jonny Laing. Good for the wildlife, he says, to leave the trees and surrounding foliage as undisturbed as possible.

What if it's a squatter? Some poor homeless person who comes over and spends their nights in the cottage. That would make sense, particularly on wet nights like this one. Maybe I should turn around. Maybe I should leave it be, because if there is a squatter, what harm are they doing? The cottage is just a roof going to waste.

I'm still searching for that rational explanation. Clawing at the void, desperate for answers.

The pale yellowy light seeps through the window. There's no movement there, not that I can make out. Beyond the cottage, darkness takes over. The fields. The woods. I don't want to bump into whatever lives in that darkness. No stags, no eagles, no nothing.

I stare at the old building.

Why would a squatter keep the light on?

I come to a stop ten metres away from the cottage door. There's a sudden rush of light-headedness. A floating sensation and, for a moment, I can't feel my feet on the long, damp grass. *Get your shit together, Angie.* The cottage is a benign, rather sad-looking building by day, but in the dark it becomes something else. Something ominous, especially with that light on. The light that shouldn't be there.

I shiver as the cold rain runs down the back of my neck.

What do I do now?

My eyes are glued to the window. I can see into the living room, and from where I'm standing, it looks empty. I'm reluctant to get too close, but how will I know if someone's in there unless I do something? I have to knock on the door. Or do I call out and hope they hear me over the wind and rain?

They?

Who's they?

I take a deep breath and fight off the instinct that wants me to leave this place. That wants me to turn around and run back to the safety of the big house so that I can wake up safe in the morning and tell myself stories that'll make me feel better. Tell myself that it was a dream. Squatter. Gardener. Cleaner. Any dream will do.

But I'm still here. Still standing in the rain, listening for something inside the house to confirm my fears. Footsteps, voices, anything.

November fifteenth.

Here you are, Angie. Standing in front of a window again. Waiting for something terrible to happen.

It's the waiting that becomes too much. I cup my hands over my mouth. Call out in a voice that sounds like it's shrunk to that of a seven-year-old child.

"Is anyone there?"

Go away, Angie. You don't want to see this.

"HELLO! Is anyone in there?"

I wish I'd gone to Nineties Madness. Why didn't I just go with them? Why didn't I just go and allow myself to have a good time?

"Hello?"

Nothing. I knew there was a rational explanation for this, and I'll be sure to ask for it from the Laings in the morning. But that's enough standing in the rain for one night. I don't like this. I want to go back to the house, where I'll be pouring myself another glass of wine. A big one. Big two. If Dan calls me back, I'll tell him I just wanted to check in and see if he was having a good time.

I turn my back on the cottage, ready to walk away.

"*Angie.*"

My pulse quickens. It sounds like a deep groan coming from inside the belly of the cottage. I have no idea if it's real or my imagination. If it's real, I have no idea if it's human or not. The old building calls to me. Like a living thing, it's summoning me back.

"Angie."

I clench both hands into tight fists. Very slowly, I turn around and see someone moving in the cottage. A human shape walking towards the window.

"Angie," says the shape.

I know that voice. I can hear it so clearly over the rain.

A wave of light engulfs the shadowy figure at the window. My legs buckle underneath me. I blink hard, clawing at my face to wipe the rainwater out of my eyes. Something pulls me towards the cottage, and I'm floating again. Not walking, floating. Closer, closer. It's clear now – the hair, the face and the voice at the window.

It's her.
It's Mum.

CHAPTER TWENTY-FOUR

I'm a seven-year-old girl standing in front of the window. Standing in front of our nice, detached house in the suburbs, where nothing bad ever happens.

Mum is standing at the window. She's too far gone, and I know what's about to happen. I know she'll set herself on fire, burn herself alive and take the nice house that she inherited from her parents with her. She doesn't want to live. She doesn't want to leave behind any trace of her existence, except for me.

Little Angie will see everything. Little Angie can't stop it. She'll live with that sight and the sound of those screams for the rest of her life. She'll run from that date on the calendar like it's a wild bear chasing after her in the woods. Every year, it'll become fresh again in her mind. Every year unless ... unless she can stop it.

"Mum?"

The cold Highland rain slaps my face, pulling me back to the present. That first November fifteenth is gone. I'm not a child in suburbia anymore. I'm in Glencoe, a forty-year-old woman standing outside an old cottage behind the Laing house. And somehow, Mum is here. I'm looking at her right now through the window. She's inside the cottage, and what else could this be if not a second chance to save her? I'm not a child. I'm strong enough to pull her out of there, out of the fire.

"Mum!"

I slip on the wet grass as I explode into a run. I thrust my arms out to retain balance and keep going until I'm at the door, grabbing the handle. Its jagged surface cuts into my skin. I pull it down. The door opens, and a groan comes from the dry, rusted hinges.

"Mum, where are you?"

I'm inside the cottage, out of the rain. No flames, no fire, yet a vicious heat burns in my mind. I wipe the rain off my face, out of my eyes as if that will help me see more clearly. Where is she? The room is a blur until my vision clears. The run-down interior and sad old furniture look the same as last time. The musty smell is the same. As is the stink of piss. And there on the floor, beside the uninviting marshmallow couch, is the Mickey Mouse cup. Someone has moved it.

"Welcome home, Angie darling."

The voice comes from behind me.

I spin around as the front door slams shut. A rasping laugh in my ear. I'm no longer in a world where my mum has miraculously come back from the dead. Where I have a second chance as a grown woman to save her.

I scream.

Martha stands with her back against the door. Her blonde hair is styled like Mum's in one of the old photos: the centre parting, the straight layers with curly ends. The geometric sixties-era dress she's wearing is covered in swirling circles and triangles. The dress strangles her body, like it's two sizes too small for her.

She grins, showing off her peg teeth.

"Welcome home, sweetheart."

I can't move.

I can't breathe or feel my legs underneath me.

She rushes – *scurries* – across the floor towards me. *Can't move. Can't breathe.* Her arm shoots up, and I don't even have time to register what she's got in her hand. *Can't move. Can't breathe.* It comes down, and although I register a split second of impact, I feel nothing. There's no pain – only the sensation of floating in an ocean of swirling circles and triangles.

That and the sound of raspy laughter.

"MUM?"

A pinprick of light in the dark. I race towards it, and the closer I get, the more everything slows down, becomes heavier and much more painful. Whatever dream I was in congeals into a harsh reality. My eyes open. I blink to a throbbing pain in my skull that feels like there's an elephant kicking a bass drum in my head.

There's a sluggish groan. I think it comes from me.

"Uggghhh."

Fortunately, my memory is intact. Unfortunately, what I remember is humiliating. How could I have fallen for it? How could I have believed, even for a minute, that I was standing at the window, watching Mum all over again?

Mum is dead. There is no saving her. All these years, I should have been saving myself when I was hiding instead.

The smell of mould and piss in the cottage is rampant. I cough so violently it's like I'm having a seizure. Then my head flops back onto the mushy couch. The smell is seeping out of the walls and roof. The marshmallow couch stinks too. My limbs are heavy. At first, I think I'm cuffed or bound with rope, but after shifting onto my side, I see that my arms are free. I'm just so out of it that it feels like being cuffed. My limbs aren't coherent. I'm like a sponge that's been squeezed dry, not a speck of strength or energy left in me.

Martha is here. She's HERE. Didn't you always know it? Deep down. Get up. GET UP!

RUN!

But I can't respond to the screaming voice in my head that blares like a siren on a loop. The blurriness in front of me is like a mist clearing, and that blurriness was Martha's face all along. She's leaning over me on the couch. I blink hard, batting away an explosion of dancing white stars. I think she's gained weight since I last saw her. Her face looks fuller, which makes the black-dot eyes even scarier.

"Wakey, wakey, sleepyhead," she says in a soft voice like she's looking down on a newborn child in a crib. "Mummy's here."

I cough so hard I almost black out again.

"Wake up," she repeats more harshly now. "Don't go back to sleep."

I make a feeble effort to lift my head off the couch so that Martha doesn't hit me again. That effort makes the room spin, and the edge of my vision starts to blur again. One thing that does catch my eye while I still have the ability to focus is a wooden truncheon on an old coffee table. Looks like an old-fashioned police truncheon. Is that what she knocked me out with?

Every time I try to move my body upwards, it feels like I'm sinking deeper into the quicksand couch. The effort drains me. I gag on the smell of this place.

"That was so much easier than I thought," she says.

Martha's examining me like I'm something trapped inside a jar. The stench of alcohol wafting off her skin is like the tip of a sharp knife poking at my temples. The closer she gets, the worse it is.

She takes a step back and straightens up. Still grinning, she pulls off the blonde wig and drops it on the floor. Her head is shaved to the bone, showing off the incredible, shocking roundness of her head.

Martha puts her glasses on. Still the same old Coke-bottle lenses that make her eyes shrink further.

"How's the head, sweetie?"

"What ... what are you doing to me?"

"Isn't it obvious?"

I can't take my eyes off that dress. Martha must have studied photos of Mum in the album she stole, memorising the typical outfits and hairstyles that made Mum look like Mum. I envision her walking into a retro clothes shop and asking for a "sixties dress". Searching for the right wig. Shaving her head to ensure a better fit. All the while, planning her revenge. She's waited a full year for this moment, and in the end, the restraining order didn't work. It just made Martha alter her tactics.

"You won't get away with it," I say. "There are other people here ... there are—"

"I know exactly who's here," she says. "I've been watching. I've been watching for days."

I get another whiff of alcohol. This time from her breath as she leans in closer.

"Didn't think I had it in me, did you? You're just like all the others, Angie dear. You think I'm a raging bull with no finesse. No patience."

I grimace, both at the smell of her breath and at my own stupidity. Did I really have some out-of-body experience that took me back to being seven, petrified and unable to help Mum? It feels stupid now. I can't explain what happened when I saw the shape of a woman at the window dressed as Mum. That sudden rush of energy and hope. The foolish hope that my entire adult life after that first November fifteenth had been a *this-is-what-will-happen* flash-forward. And that I was back there. That I could stop it. That I could change everything.

"Answer me, Angie."

"W-w-what?"

"You didn't think I had it in me, did you? That's your problem. That's *everyone's* problem. You all underestimated me."

She screams with laughter. The pain in my head is so sharp it feels like someone is pulling my teeth out with pliers.

Martha grabs a silver hip flask off the coffee table. She takes a swig and pulls a face like she just drank vinegar mixed with washing-up liquid. She screws the lid back on, lowers the flask onto the table next to the truncheon. Then she walks back to the couch, her footsteps heavy slaps off the floor.

"Oh, if only you'd just gone through with the holiday last year," she says, still giggling to herself. "You wouldn't have come home early. You'd have been none the wiser, and none of this would've happened. Even if it did happen and you'd been just a little nicer, it still wouldn't have happened."

She lowers her voice to a whisper.

"Did you really think I would just go away, Angie? That I'd let you get away with how you treated me?"

I don't answer. Can't answer.

"That wasn't my first restraining order, Angie dear."

"Martha—"

"Thought you were clever," she snarls. "Didn't you? So you went digging. So you found William and listened to the bullshit ramblings of a dying old man. His brain is riddled with cancer, did you know that? He's off his head. Doesn't know what he's talking about. Doesn't know his own name half the time."

I have no idea if Martha's telling the truth. Behind her, I notice the light bulb in the main socket on the ceiling. Has she been taking the bulb in and out? Has she been putting it on every night since we've been here, calling to me?

"How would you react, Angie? If Dan was screwing your best friend. If the two people you trusted most in the world were laughing behind your back – what would you do?"

"Martha, please—"

"And he said I'M the monster?"

"Please—"

Her voice is a bark. "Shut up. You're not in control, Angie dear. You never were."

Staying on top of all this is hard work, and it's draining what little battery I have left. Martha's face is a blur again. Sometimes I see three Marthas, their faces distorted and the bald heads shining above me. It feels like I'm drowning in the couch, but I know I need to hold on. God knows what she'll do to me if I black out.

"Please don't," I say. "Don't do this."

She's close to my face again. Her breath, a gust of pure vodka. I go cold as she kisses me on the lips, a clumsy peck that feels like a humid swamp enveloping my head. Then she's back in the middle of the room, pounding her chest like a gorilla. Yelling in a voice that's like a chainsaw in my ear.

"I am a MOTHER, and I have the right to see my son and grandchild. Those bastards have poisoned my boy's mind against me and robbed me of being a part of their lives. They've been doing it for years. YEARS."

She grabs the wooden truncheon off the table. Paces the room, hitting it repeatedly against the palm of her hand.

"People think they can dismiss me, Angie. Dismiss the stupid old bitch and she'll go away. Hmm? Like I'm some kind of *thing* that's outlived its usefulness. Don't you see? William wasn't innocent. Sadie wasn't innocent, and she got what she deserved. No more pretty little angel wiggling her tight little arse in her tight jeans for the boys. They couldn't see past her face, not until I made a few improvements. Cruel? No. It was justice, a just punishment."

The truncheon is a blur as it whacks off her palm, which is now red and angry. If she keeps going, that hand will be twice its normal size in the morning.

"WHORE! WHORE! WHORE!"

How is no one else hearing this?

Then I remember where we are. No other houses for miles.

"William's a whore too! He always liked the pretty little women with their tight little arses. Women like Sadie. Women like ... like *you*."

She stops pacing and points the truncheon at me. Her voice is a crackling hiss.

"Is that how you got him to talk, Angie dear? Did you wiggle your little arse for the decrepit old fucker? Did you make him feel young one last time?"

She puts the truncheon down. Takes another manic swig from the hip flask.

"Maybe I should cut your face up."

I'm about to protest, but she's wagging a finger back and forth. Telling me no. The laughter that follows is lethargic and less hysterical. Sounds like the vodka is slowing her down.

"Don't worry, Angie. I've got something much better planned for you."

She sits down on one of the old chairs, her chest heaving. The chair wobbles on uneven legs.

"You were so close to finding me the other day," she says, the grin returning to her reddening face. "I wasn't expecting visitors, but, lucky me, I saw you approaching from the house. Oh, you gave me a fright. I hid my crisps and Coke behind the couch. Then I ran out the back door and hid there. But I forgot the cup, didn't I? Oh, Angie, you were in the kitchen. I was watching you through the back window. You came so close to ruining the surprise. So … *close*."

"How did you know I was here?" I ask.

She looks at me. Her voice is cold and flat.

"I've been following you, Angie. We've got unfinished business."

She slaps her knee, and her eyes light up. "Oh, by the way, your new house sitter isn't all she's cracked up to be."

Panic swells inside me. "What did you do to her?"

Martha shakes her head, looking at me like I'm an imbecile. "Relax. I didn't touch her. But did you know she leaves the front door unlocked when she goes into the back garden with Billie Jean and Brogan? That's careless. Someone might sneak in. Someone might leave something in your secret drawer. Underneath Mummy's photo album."

"Leave what?"

"A letter."

I battle through the mental fog. "What letter? What are you talking about?"

She stands up and walks around the back of the couch. Seconds later, she's leaning over me again, holding up a piece of A4 paper. There's something typed on the front. Looks like a short note.

"What's that?" I ask.

"You should know, Angie. You wrote it."

"What ...?"

"There are two versions of this letter," Martha says, still leaning over me on the couch. "This one right here. And the other one that I left in your house."

I strain my eyes, trying to make sense of the black squiggles on the paper. The squiggles shimmer and dance. I can't make out a single word. "What is it?"

Martha sits down on the edge of the couch. Then she clears her throat.

"This, Angie dear, is a very sad letter. This is a letter that a grief-stricken Dan will find when he goes home and starts clearing out your things. Maybe he'll start in your top drawer, lift up the photo album, and that's when he'll find the other version of this letter. This is your goodbye – your sorrowful farewell after years of anguish about your mum's death. You've been planning it for a long time, haven't you? It states specifically what you're going to do to yourself. This is how you believe you'll be reunited with your mum."

I try to sit up, fighting the lead weight in my stomach.

"Martha, don't."

Martha gets up, and I hear her joints popping. She disappears around the back of the couch again, but I can just about see her as she reaches for something. When she straightens up, she's holding a red jerry can. She gives it a shake, and I can hear the liquid sloshing around inside.

"Yes, I had to be patient. And I had a feeling you and Dan would go somewhere around dear Mummy's anniversary. Seeing as how it didn't go so well last year. Luckily for me, it wasn't Spain or Australia. But I was ready. Oh, I've been ready for a long time. And so I followed you all the way up here."

She cackles, and it's a dry, hacking sound.

"Martha—"

"Thank God for this little cottage," she says. "It was perfect for keeping watch. It's also perfect for those rich boys too, because we don't have to burn that big, beautiful house down, do we? We can do it all here."

Move. Run. Stop her.

I let out a scream inside. My useless body can't or won't obey the commands of my brain. I can't move. I'm helpless, and I'm at the mercy of a madwoman.

Martha clicks her fingers to get my attention. When she has it, she points to a box of matches on the table. She never takes her eyes off me.

"Are you ready, Angie dear? Are you ready to go see Mummy?"

CHAPTER TWENTY-FIVE

"Martha," I plead. My voice is a strangled gasp for air. "Please stop. Please don't do this."

I manage to sit up on the couch. The white stars are back, but I stand up anyway, pushing myself onto my feet. I feel like a drunk on a merry-go-round. Martha, the predator, is watching my every move. I stagger forward with my hands up in surrender, then drop onto my knees in front of her.

I clasp my hands, head bowed. Praying to her like she's a god.

"I'm sorry. I'm ... so sorry."

Martha's voice cuts like a razor. She looks down at me with something that, I hope, almost resembles pity. "Stupid child."

"Please ... don't ... kill me."

"Oh, Angie dear, your fate was sealed the moment you decided to humiliate me last year. It was always going to end badly for you."

My throat feels like there's a knot in it. I'm sweating bullets.

"I didn't mean to."

"That's the problem with people these days," Martha says. "No one wants to face the consequences of their actions. But there *are* consequences to treating me the way you've all been treating me. And right now, I'll start with you, Angie."

Will Dan believe it? That I left a suicide note at home? That I was planning to do something to myself all this time?

Something. You know what she's going to do.

What does it matter if he believes it? He'll have to live with it whether he believes or not. The same way I've had to live with what happened to Mum.

My hands are still tightly clasped together. A ball of ten fingers, trembling violently. "I'm sorry. I'm sorry for what I did. Please don't kill me."

Martha swirls the petrol around inside the jerry can. Slowly. I hear that sloshing sound again, and I know it's for me. She's dragging this out, enjoying every second of it.

"Stop begging, Angie. Besides, you're going out in a blaze of glory. People are going to see the smoke for miles."

I unclasp my fingers. Hold my hands up, palms outwards. Classic surrender pose.

"Wait."

"Wait?"

"Martha, I need to tell you something. It's important. It's something I should've told you from the start."

She shakes the can.

Splosh-splosh.

"Save it."

"It explains *why* I did what I did. Why I humiliated you when we came back last year. In other words, why all this happened in the first place."

"No."

"It matters, Martha."

Her eyes narrow. "What do you want to tell me, sweetie? That you're sorry again? Haven't you learned by now I'm not interested? Do you think that's why I followed you all the way up here? For a word?"

Holy shit, I think. She really is going to burn me alive in this cottage and make it look like suicide. This is not a bluff. She's right. She hasn't followed me all the way up here for a word. Hidden in the cottage, shaved her head and dressed up as my mum. That wasn't for nothing. That wasn't for *sorry*. She's watched and waited. Now I've walked straight into her arms.

"We didn't come back early because Dan wasn't feeling well," I say. "It had nothing to do with that. That was just something Dan and I made up on the way back. I never told you the real reason because … because …"

She rattles the can. *Splosh-splosh.*

"What are you talking about, Angie?"

"We didn't tell you," I say, looking up at her, "because it's very personal. Because it's embarrassing."

It's my last throw of the dice, so I keep talking. "Dan said something about you on our first night away. When we were at Loch Lomond. Something that I couldn't handle. Something that made me feel … *jealous*."

Martha is still, but I see it. I see her eyes light up with expectation as she looks down at me. "What did he say?"

I wipe a bead of sweat off my face. "I couldn't believe that he said it."

She takes a step forward.

"Said what?"

I pause for breath. "We were sitting in the hotel restaurant, the one at Loch Lomond. It was just a *stupid* game we were playing. It wasn't supposed to … it wasn't supposed to go anywhere. It definitely wasn't supposed to bring our holiday to an end."

This all sounds like childish drivel. But Martha hasn't blinked in about a minute. She's *listening*.

"Game?"

I nod. "Yes."

"What game?"

"Snog, marry or avoid."

She pulls a face. "Snog … what?"

"It's a stupid game that people play," I tell her. "Have you heard of it? It's a light-hearted version of kiss, marry, kill."

Martha looks at me like I'm speaking Russian. I'm losing her.

"I'm trying to explain why I was so angry at you," I say.

She curls her lip at me. "Explain."

"You pick three people in the game," I say. "They can be fictional or real. One you'd kiss for, I don't know, a casual thing. One you'd marry for a long-term relationship. And the third you'd avoid – or kill."

Martha inches closer. "You put *me* in this game?"

I nod, trying not to flinch at her vodka-blast breath. "We'd had a few drinks. It was harmless. It was *supposed* to be harmless."

She leans over me, narrowing her little dot eyes in concentration. "What did he say about me? What did he say, Angie sweetheart?"

I bury my face in my hands. My voice is thick and muffled as I shake my head. I mumble gibberish, and Martha swats my hands away from my face. Her eyes swell up, bulging with curiosity. She no longer wants to know. She *needs* to know.

"What did he say?" she asks, her voice spiralling in pitch. "What did he say about me?"

She leans in closer, hungry for information. I've got both hands on the floor, and I feel like a sprinter on the blocks. Crouched. Ready to push off. Ready to go.

Splosh-slosh-splosh.

"WHAT DID HE SAY?"

She gasps. Then slowly, she grins at me.

"Did he say ... *marry*?" Martha squeals with excitement. "He did, didn't he? Oh, I knew it. I knew there was a little electricity there the first time I walked into your house. He couldn't keep his eyes off me, could he? Sorry, Angie, but not every man likes the stick-insect look, do they? Men just know. They know a woman who can please them."

She's almost fully closed the gap between us. Something that I never could have done on my own, especially not down on my knees like this. Not before she'd have me covered in petrol. Struck a match. *Whoosh.*

"That's why I was so angry at you," I say.

She nods, smooths her hands down over her breasts. "Thank you for your confession. It won't save you, but I do want to know what he said about me, Angie. Was it snog or marry?"

She stares at me with those tiny unblinking eyes.

"Well?"

I whisper, "He said ..."

She comes closer. "Speak up."

"He said ..."

Another step forward and I know I'll never get this chance again. I make a grab for the jerry can. But I miss, and there's a split second of *oh shit, I've blown it*. My grasping hand slams into Martha's forearm with so much force that I rock her to the bone. She lets out an ear-piercing shriek and drops the jerry can on the floor.

"Bitch!"

Martha stares at me, her eyes burning with hatred. The jerry can has tipped onto its side. Martha already removed the lid, and now there's a steady stream of petrol leaking across the floor.

"No!" she cries, noticing the spill.

Now she goes for the can instead of me. I throw myself at her, and we fall backwards. Martha's glasses topple off her face as we hit the deck. She lands on her spine and makes a high-pitched howling noise. I dig a knee into her stomach, and although she winces in acknowledgement of the blow, it doesn't slow her down. She clamps her stubby hands on both sides of my head. Her face is a burning red orb. Hatred spilling out of her black eyes. She locks down her grip and starts squeezing my head inwards. A wheezing sound shoots out of me. White stars, black stars, red stars flood my vision. The pain is so intense that I'm convinced I'll black out at any second. I grip her arms, trying to loosen the grip. Jesus, she's strong. It's like trying to push an oak tree out of the way.

I can smell the petrol on the floor. Suddenly it's the only smell in the cottage.

For some reason, I picture Dan in his silly baggy tracksuit at Nineties Madness. I think about how much fun he's having and how I wish that I'd gone with him instead of walking into Martha's trap.

It's the thought of Dan that encourages me to fight off Martha's python-like grip. I find the strength to push her arms back. A gap opens, and my head, soaked with sweat, slips free. The lights come back on, but I'm running on emergency batteries, and there's definitely not much left in those. Martha isn't willing to let me go so easily. She shows surprising speed and grabs me again with both hands. We're back in the same position. She squeezes harder on my head this time. Trying to pop me like a zit on prom night.

The world goes dark.

Acceptance begins to seep in. I'm going to die. There's no way of stopping this.

Martha climbs up to a knee, still holding my head in her hands. She drags me across the floor. My feet slip, and I battle to retain a solid footing. She stops and tightens her grip. Then I feel it. Her thumbs sliding up over my cheeks. She's searching for my eyes. She wants to gouge them out.

I feel a jolt of terror.

"No," I say in a mangled voice.

She stabs at the outer edges of my eye sockets. Searching for the fleshy bits. I close my eyes. Try to lower my head and stay out of range of her jabbing thumbs. Her nails dig in, piercing the skin around my eyes. There's an explosion of pain. I feel a trickle of warm blood running down my face. She's too strong. I can't keep her off.

I gamble, lashing out with my fists. I throw wild punches at what I hope is Martha's head. It's like punching a brick wall, and my hands explode with pain as I hit the back of her skull. But one shot – a left hook – connects flush with Martha's jaw. I feel the bones in my arm shudder. She cries out. Her legs buckle.

I wriggle free of her death grip for a second time.

"Bitch!" she yells, a hand pressed against her face. She takes the hand off and checks for blood.

The world is spinning faster than ever. I can just about feel my legs underneath me. Then I see it – the truncheon on the table.

I make a move to grab it. Martha does too, and she's faster and less disorientated than I am. Her feet make a hurried scraping noise on the floor as she covers the gap to the table. She snatches the truncheon up and holds it mid-air, ready to strike.

I freeze.

That's Rita in front of me now. She's a monster, and if she knocks me out, I won't wake up. Or if I do, I'll be on fire.

Her chest heaves as she fights for breath. The truncheon is up, ready to strike, and despite her breathlessness, she grins at me. Shows me a wall of bloody shark teeth.

"Just so you know, I'll let Dan suffer for a while when this is over. Then he'll have an accident. I'll leave some rat poison out for your cat and dog. You'll all be together again soon, Angie. One happy little family in the cemetery."

Her laughter is insane.

She takes a step towards me, wielding the truncheon overhead. Her eyes glaze over, and she's so focused on me that she isn't noticing where her feet are treading.

"Goodbye, Angie. Say hi to your mum for—"

Her lead foot skates through the puddle on the floor, and there's a noise like a fork squeaking over a plate. Martha gasps. Her left leg shoots out in a forward lunging motion. The truncheon slips out of her hand, landing with a thud on the wet floor.

Her eyes flash with panic. She looks at me. Reaches for me, instinctively seeking help.

"Ohhhhhggh."

She jerks back and forth. Her left foot skids on the petrol again, and she topples over onto her back. It's a hard slam against the floor. A loud crack as her skull takes the worst of the fall. She's still for a second, and I'm sure she's dead. Convinced of it. Then her head starts rolling from side to side in slow motion. She makes a dull wheezing sound, and her eyes roll back.

I watch as Martha's chubby legs make some kind of drunken walking motion on the ground. There's some part of her brain that thinks she's still on her feet.

I notice the rain outside for the first time in an age. A quiet pitter-patter in my ears. Tapping off the window. Everything else blurs. There's only Martha and me. And I'll never be free of this woman unless I do something that, at any other point in my life, would be beyond me.

I lift the matches off the table, taking care to avoid getting petrol on my shoes. Not an easy task in my condition. But my hands don't shake as I slide the tray out. Not even when I take a match from inside.

Martha lifts her bald head off the floor. Blood spills from the back of her skull, leaking onto the floor. Still, she seems alert. Her eyes widen with terror when she sees the box of matches in my hand. Her nostrils twitch. She sniffs the air and inhales the sweet-smelling petrol.

"Angie, darling," she slurs, "what are you doing?"

I strike the match. Hold the little flame aloft and watch as it burns slowly down to my fingertips.

Martha lets loose a hysterical, shuddering laugh. "Oh,

Angie! I wasn't going to do it. I ... I was just trying to scare you."

She looks at me. Blood spilling from her mouth, nose and head. Her manic grin slowly fizzles out.

"I'm not a monster," she says. "Believe me. I wasn't going to do it. I'm *not* a monster, Angie, whatever they say."

I feel the heat at my fingers. Just enough time for a final glance at Martha, giving her an indifferent shrug.

"But I am."

I drop the match onto the floor.

"ANNNNGIIEEE!"

I turn and sprint towards the door. There's a deep whooshing noise that rushes up from the floor. I *feel* it, like an explosion under the cottage.

Martha screams, and I'll never forget that sound for as long as I live. The scream of a wild animal, accompanied by a cacophony of noise. Crashing and banging sounds that chase me out of the cottage. I reach the door, aware of the soaring heat behind me.

I grab the handle. Something makes me look over my shoulder.

Martha is a ball of flames with arms and legs. Somehow, she's up on her feet. She's chasing after me, her flailing arms reaching for me. She makes one last run towards the door. Towards me.

"ANNNNGIIEEE!"

I pull the handle and hurl myself outside. Slam the door shut just in time to hear a colossal thud on the other side. Then a dull, thumping noise as Martha collapses against it from the inside. One more gargled scream. My name was in that scream.

I keep my back pressed up tight against the door. I'm not

sure how long I stay there for. Waiting. Waiting for Martha in flames to burst through the door, still chasing me. Still intent on making me pay. I wait and wait and wait. But nothing more happens.

When I'm sure she won't come after me, I take my back off the door and walk onto the grass. Then I turn around and watch the old cottage burn.

EPILOGUE

"And the winner of this year's Silver Revolver award for the best newcomer in Scottish crime fiction goes to ..."

The next part is a blur. I sit in my seat in the small theatre, my sweaty hand locked in Dan's grip. He's squeezing tight. I'm squeezing back so hard there's a good chance I might break his bones. I can't believe where I am tonight.

The old man with the shock of white hair at the podium, some kind of publishing bigwig, says something. A name – it must be a name. That's what he's up there for, to announce the winner.

The words are lost on me.

I don't want to win, I tell myself. And right now, I don't. It's an honour to have been longlisted, shortlisted and invited to the awards ceremony here in this beautiful Edinburgh arts venue. That's good enough for me. More than good enough. Anyway, I can't possibly win. I'm up against some exceptional people here, and I don't want to go up on that stage and make a fool of myself. I'm not sure I belong here.

The room is bursting with applause, the floor trembling

beneath all of us. Some people are up on their feet, looking around and waiting for the winner to make an appearance. To make the walk to glory.

I don't hear my name when it's called out. I don't hear the name of my book either, but Dan does, and he's pulling me up off my seat by the arm and pointing towards the stage that might as well be a million miles away from our seats. He mouths two words at me – *you won*. I don't know if he's kidding or not, but there are a lot of people looking at me. Smiling. Saying things I don't hear or understand.

"You did it," Dan says, throwing his arms around me. He pulls back, and there are tears streaming down his face, and that almost sets me off too. Then he points towards the stage.

"Go. Go on, Angie. You won!"

I walk or float towards the stage with the sound of applause ringing in my ears. Will it ever stop? I've got high heels on, and I'm wearing a fancy red dress. After months of working in tracksuit bottoms and hoodies covered in pet hair, I feel like a freak. A freak who's forgotten how to put one foot in front of the other.

This is real. It's really happening.

I won.

The applause is still going when I reach the podium. It's hard to figure out how I got here in the seven months since the book's release. Luck smiled on me, I guess. The novel was well received, first by the publisher, who was excited to work with me after I showed them the manuscript. More work followed. Tweaking. Editing. Cover art. Promo and then somewhere down the line, release day came, and readers loved it. They loved my book – the book I'd toiled over, cried over, doubted, hated and thought about throwing in the bin more times than I can count. The book took off at a startling speed. It got picked by several podcasts as their book of the month, and from there the train just kept rolling. BookTubers and BookTok helped spread the word. I'm lucky, I know that. I *know* that. Some writers toil away in the shadows and never receive any recognition for their work.

I shake the old man's hand, and he offers me the little gun-shaped award. I'm laughing because it's so heavy.

Speech. Now I've got to give a speech.

It's here. I've got it here. The piece of paper in my hand; it'll be a miracle if I don't drop it.

I clear my throat and take in the room. All those faces under the lights. They're all looking at me, and at last, the venue falls silent.

You have to say something.

"I can't believe this is happening," I say, leaning into the mic. My voice sounds huge and overamplified, like it's coming down from the heavens.

"I'd like to dedicate this award to the memory of my mum, who passed away a long time ago. She taught me so much in the short time that we had together. Not a day goes by when I don't think of you, Mum. I miss you. I love you. This is for you."

That earns me another round of applause, and it's also when I feel a sudden gust of warmth, a sudden *heat*, drifting up from the seats towards the stage. This feeling is so powerful that, for a moment, I forget what I'm doing and look out at the sea of faces in front of me.

I almost drop the award.

Martha Hunt is sitting in the middle of the theatre. Middle row, middle seat. She's almost directly in line with the podium where I'm standing now. The colours on her flowery cardigan shine brighter than ever, dazzling me like a convoy of trucks with their headlights on full beam. Her hair has sprouted back into a perm, and even from where I'm standing on the stage, I can tell she's grinning at me, showing off those predatory teeth. The Coke-bottle glasses swallow up most of her face.

"Umm ..."

There's an excruciating silence, and if a pin dropped on the floor, it would sound like a nuclear explosion. I'm paralysed. I can't think, and my tongue is a giant fleshy knot in my mouth. Fortunately, I manage to snap out of it. I get on with the speech. I thank my agent, publisher, Dan, and anyone else I can think of. But I'm as stiff as a board, the words coming out a little too high-pitched and manic.

The lights go up when it's over. The old man takes my arm and starts to lead me off the stage to the sound of rapturous applause.

Martha Hunt is dead. I know that for a fact. The police confirmed it after the fire in Glencoe, and I've got no reason to doubt it. I saw her covered in flames. I watched that old cottage burn to a shell. There's no way anyone could have survived that, and there's no way she's sitting in the audience tonight.

It's impossible.

One last glance. Just to be sure. But the old man is a fast walker, a *really* fast walker, and looking over my shoulder, slightly off-balance, I can't see towards the audience clearly anymore. Everything's a blur again. My eyes are frantic as I search for the middle row, middle seat, just to confirm what I already know. And I *do* know it. That she's dead. Martha Hunt is dead.

All of a sudden we're in a backstage area, filled with a wall of smiling faces, big hugs and endless congratulations.

White light beams down from the ceiling, and it's like being trapped inside a giant vivarium. A glass of champagne is thrust into my hand. A woman comes over and wants me to sign a copy of my book. I sign it and hand it back to her, all the while checking over my shoulder. Checking this way, that way. Watching the doorway. Wondering where the nearest fire exit is.

And that's the rest of my night. I stand in the dressing room, clutching my award in one hand and a glass of champagne in the other.

Watching the door. Waiting for the house sitter to come back.

THE END

THANK YOU FOR READING

Did you enjoy reading *While You Were Gone*? Please consider leaving a review on Amazon. Your review will help other readers to discover the novel.

ABOUT THE AUTHOR

Mark Gillespie writes psychological thriller and suspense novels. He's a former professional musician (bass player) from Glasgow, Scotland who spent ten years touring the UK and Ireland, playing sessions and having the time of his life. Don't ask though. What happened on the road stays on the road.

He now lives in Auckland, New Zealand with his wife and a small menagerie of rescue creatures. If he's not writing, he's jamming with other musicians, running on the beach, watching mixed martial arts and boxing. Or devouring horror and thriller movies.

www.markgillespieauthor.com

ALSO BY MARK GILLESPIE

I Know Who You Are
The Lost Girl
Fool Me Once
While You Were Gone

Printed in Dunstable, United Kingdom